A DEADLY VENETIAN AFFAIR

HENRY FLEMING INVESTIGATES

BOOK FOUR

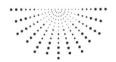

JAY GILL

VISIT WWW.JAYGILL.NET

WELCOME NOTE

Welcome, readers old and new. I'm excited to share with you a most challenging investigation for private detective Henry Fleming entitled *A Deadly Venetian Affair*.

This mystery is set in the 1920s and although it's part of a series, each case can be read as a standalone. In addition, within the pages you will find no graphic violence, bedroom shenanigans or strong language.

These stories are spoiler-free and, in the best tradition of the whodunnit, the cast of suspects, along with a smattering of red-herrings, will have you guessing until the very end when our great detective presides over his *grand reveal*.

I'm sure you're eager to uncover the truth behind what took place in Venice and so, without further delay, let's begin.

Cast List

Henry Fleming (Private detective)
Mrs Clayton (Fleming's housekeeper)
Skip (Fleming's yellow Labrador)
Dr James Ingrey
Teddy Kelleher
Elsie Kelleher
Captain Jim Maitland
Sir Ernest Templeton
Lady Templeton
Dolores Frost (Lady Templeton's companion)
Antonio Durante
Gerardo Castelli
Fern Blake
Nancy Perkins
Inspector Luigi Trotta
Signorina Lombardi (reception manageress)
Signor Rossi (hotel porter)
Pietro (maître d')
Countess Volkov

An Extract from the Diary of
H. K. Fleming, Esq.

Venice is more beautiful, and has more wonders than is fair for one city. The Venetian people are kind and generous. I'm here at the behest of Countess Volkov who has encountered some trouble. After discreet inquiries on her behalf, I've made quick progress and confirmed her fears. Together we've agreed a plan and all being well I'll complete my work swiftly and return to England in a day or two.

I was pleasantly surprised to be invited to dinner by Sir Ernest and Lady Templeton. I had sensed at the outset that there was more behind their invitation than an opportunity for us to become properly acquainted, and my intuition was correct. Having heard their story I find myself worried for them and, despite my insistence they return to England at once, they're adamant they will stay.

Having completed the case for Countess Volkov, which went like clockwork (I'm pleased to note), it appears I'm to become embroiled in an altogether different affair. One small consolation is that it gives me more time to explore this magnificent city and the sweet delights Venice has to offer. There are desserts here like nothing I've experienced before. (Of course, one must be careful not to say as much within Mrs Clayton's hearing!)

Today, at the Royale Fiore Hotel, I became better acquainted with Sir Ernest and Lady Templeton, and was introduced to Lady Templeton's companion Miss Frost. At dinner, keen to converse with as many of the guests as possible, I found my discourse with Dr James Ingrey of particular interest.

Despite my best efforts I have been caught unawares. This morning, I and the hotel's porter, discovered a body. At this moment in time, I will admit, I'm at a loss to understand the motive. Quite naturally, the hotel's guests are shocked, but until I know more of the background to this death, I cannot say with certainty whether any of them are responsible.

I have decided it prudent to enrol the assistance of Dr Ingrey. A second pair of eyes and ears has proven useful in the past. He seems an inquisitive sort of fellow and his enthusiasm more than makes up for what he so obviously lacks in investigative experience.

The case has taken a complicated and quite unexpected turn. I find myself examining a conundrum within a mystery. I fear that at the heart of this inquiry lies a dark and long hidden secret.

'Truth will come to light;
murder cannot be hid long;
a man's son may, but in the end truth will out.'
Merchant of Venice; William Shakespeare

PART I

TRUTH WILL COME TO LIGHT

CHAPTER ONE

THE BOY

As he got older they said he looked like her, although he was never really sure if that was true. Try as he might he couldn't remember; he knew her only from a photograph that had stood on the mantelpiece. When a fire was lit in the huge iron grate, her face took on a warm glow, the flickering shadows making her seem alive and, although in the photograph she isn't smiling, he would imagine her gentle eyes turning to him and her mouth curving lovingly upwards. He thought her beautiful.

Growing up, family talked about her and he was grateful, even though his heart ached with longing when he heard the stories of which he never tired.

On his mother's birthday, it was customary to dress in his church suit and he and his aunt would visit her grave. It seemed always to be such a hot day and the rough material would make him sweat and itch. By the time he was perhaps seven or eight years old, the trousers were too short and the jacket had become tight under the arms – he could no longer button it at the front. That was the year he wanted to take the jacket off but his aunt had insisted he keep it on. As in all things, he capitulated; he had no fight in him then. They said he was a quiet boy. A child that carried loss like a sack of jagged rocks on his back.

The walk was always made in silence, his aunt's hand growing tighter the closer they got. He didn't like to look at the faded headstone; that wasn't how he wanted to remember her. He preferred the photograph, the stories, and his dreams. That grey slab of stone would never be her.

Nevertheless he read the name: Sophia Maria Lavigna. A beautiful Italian name. His eyes following the shape of the letters, he'd silently mouth each word.

His aunt had passed him a bouquet of pink lilies which he cradled in his small arms. He'd stumbled forward as he went to lay them down but his aunt was in time to catch him. The heavy, cloying scent of the flowers was strong and he'd wrinkled his nose. With his aunt's encouragement he'd knelt and placed them on the grave.

He had known she'd cry; she always did. He preferred to shed his tears when alone.

His uncle never went with them. He worked long, odd hours and he'd either be at his bakery or sleeping. He liked his uncle. His jokes made everyone laugh. When his uncle kissed his aunt it made her happy. Even though she'd sometimes playfully slap him and tell him off for tickling her when she was busy.

The boy often wondered if his mother's laugh had sounded like his aunt's. They were sisters so he thought it must have been similar.

It was two years later when his uncle told him the truth about his mother's death, and what had really happened.

His aunt was furious, but he was relieved. He'd known there was something more to it and now, like all the adults, he knew too.

'The boy has a right to know the truth,' his uncle had insisted and he'd been correct. The truth had freed him.

And now, today, as he looked at his reflection in the carriage window, he saw a grown man. No longer the pliant, quiet boy he once had been.

He checked the time on his wristwatch. The train would soon depart.

The young woman in the seat opposite glanced up from her book and looked at him again.

'Let me guess,' he said. 'You're headed to Milan?'

She smiled coyly. 'Perhaps.'

'Bologna then?'

'Maybe.'

'Why would a beautiful woman be travelling alone?' He shifted along his seat so he was directly opposite her. He leaned forward and looked into her lovely green eyes. 'If you were mine I'd never allow you out of my sight. Not even for a moment.'

She giggled. 'It's a good job I'm not yours then. I'm not some little bird you can keep in a cage. And what makes you think I'm travelling alone?'

'I see no ring on your finger, nor any sight of a boyfriend, fiancé, or husband.' He was just about to continue when the carriage door opened.

'Father!' said the young woman. 'I was wondering where you'd got to. I'd hate for anyone to get the wrong idea and think I was travelling alone.' She raised an eyebrow and grinned. 'As you've told me so many times, the world is full of charmers... and chancers.'

The young man slid back along his seat, stifling laughter as he looked out of the window.

Outside on the station platform a whistle sounded, carriage doors slammed, and the signalman waved his flag.

The young woman's father lifted his trunk onto the overhead shelf. After much huffing and puffing and, just as the train lurched forward, he fell onto the seat beside his daughter, panting heavily. 'We're headed to Verona; it's where I was born. I wish for my daughter to know the city of her forebears. And you? Where are you going?'

'Venice,' he replied.

'And might I ask why you're off to Venice?'

The young man thought about the question for a moment, then said: 'I suppose you could say I'm on a pilgrimage.'

CHAPTER TWO

THE COUNTESS

Venice, Italy.

Inside St Mark's Basilica, Henry Fleming sat in silence, staring in awe at the Pala d'Oro. The Byzantine altarpiece, adorned with hundreds of exquisitely wrought enamels on sheet gold, each delicately set with glistening pearls and precious stones, the whole marvel held within a gilded silver frame, took his breath away. Nothing, neither pictures nor extensive reading, could have prepared him for the emotions now welling within. That man was capable of creating something of such wondrous beauty touched him beyond words.

Behind him, there was movement. Countess Volkov was leaving. With the aid of a walking stick, she passed through the cathedral towards the monumental bronze doors of the exit.

Fleming took one last look at the golden masterpiece before getting to his feet. Taking his time, he allowed a moment to adjust his waistcoat and jacket, to check the shine of his shoes. He waited for the countess to leave, then fell in behind the two men who followed her, noting the shorter man leaned heavily to his right, possibly due to an injury to his left side. The other, taller man, turned to talk to his limping companion, and Fleming observed a thick scar above his right eye, running from hairline to eyebrow. Their voices carried in the vastness and Fleming could make out hushed words spoken in Russian.

Fleming passed through the bronze cathedral doors into the bright sun and stifling midday heat of St Mark's Square. He donned his newly purchased Borsalino Fedora and removed his jacket, folding it neatly over his arm. Keeping his distance, he too followed in the footsteps of the countess as she crossed the square. On the far side, the Russians kept to the shadows; a pair of stalking jackals.

After ten minutes, and having entered a quiet, narrow side street, the countess stopped at a small bar to rest her aching feet. She placed her handbag on the seat beside her, ordered sweet black coffee and took out her cigarettes.

With his eyes firmly fixed on the countess, Fleming knelt down and adjusted his shoelaces. He waited. Eventually, at the far end of the narrow street, the two Russians appeared, walking slowly and nonchalantly towards the bar.

Fleming rose, threw back his shoulders and, with long purposeful strides, placed himself between the countess and the Russians, his hand firmly on the chair where the lady's handbag rested.

'Excuse me. So sorry to bother you. I'm looking for the Grand Hotel Venezia. I'm staying there but I appear to have become hopelessly lost,' he said, chuckling like a hapless tourist.

The countess looked up with surprise. Her eyes appraised Fleming, then fell on the two men approaching.

At the same moment, the bar's *cameriere* appeared. He offered a table, but Fleming only repeated his tale of being lost. The waiter pointed and waved his arms as he gave directions back to the hotel.

While he spoke, Fleming's eyes had been tracking the two Russians who had now walked on past the bar. Thanking the waiter and apologising to the countess for the intrusion, he turned and moved in the direction of his hotel. Looking up and down the narrow street, the Russians were now nowhere to be seen.

Back at the Grand Hotel Venezia, Fleming entered the lobby and approached the reception desk.

'Ah, Signor Fleming. A letter for you.' The young woman handed him an envelope.

'*Mille grazie*.' Fleming opened the envelope and read the card inside.

'Is everything okay, signor?'

'Yes, thank you. I'll be dining with company this evening. It seems Sir Ernest and Lady Templeton have booked a table in the restaurant here and would like me to join them.' He took out his pocket watch and checked the time. 'I must hurry. I wish to get to the restaurant early. I need to speak to Pietro, the maître d', before dinner commences. Would you be so kind as to notify them that I'd be delighted to accept their invitation?'

He was heading for the hotel's wide sweeping staircase when he observed Countess Volkov entering the lift. He changed direction and joined her.

Henry Fleming's eyes searched the dining room of the Grand Hotel Venezia. He recognised celebrities, aristocrats, and politicians from many nations, all enjoying first-class food and service in one of the most fashionable hotels in the world. He noted one eminent politician with his mistress, who would inform anyone who enquired that she was nothing more than his personal assistant. However, to Fleming, the signs were obvious. Their eyes revealed all. As did the shoes and earrings. Theirs was no business meeting. No personal assistant wears such expensive shoes to work unless wanting to impress. The diamond earrings were most certainly a recent gift from her lover, again inappropriate as work attire, and worn for him to show her appreciation.

Every table in the restaurant of Grand Hotel Venezia was occupied. The room bristled with the world's elite. When he'd arrived, he'd encountered several friends and acquaintances, who'd wished to greet him and shake his hand. He'd had to apologise several times to Sir Ernest and Lady Templeton for the interruptions. Her ladyship though appeared fascinated by the attention Fleming attracted and felt validated in her decision to ask the renowned detective to join them for dinner.

'Is everything to your liking?' she asked. 'Is there something wrong with your *gelato*?'

Beside one of two marble pillars that rose from floor to ceiling, the two Russians sat at a table attempting to blend in with the other guests. They now wore suits and were clean shaven except for fashionable moustaches. They hadn't touched their drinks and had made little inroad on their main courses. Every so often, one or other of them would glance towards Countess Volkov who sat unaccompanied at a small table at the back of the restaurant.

'The dessert is perfect. It's magnificent,' said Fleming. 'My apologies, I give you my word that you will shortly have my full attention. Please excuse me, I require a discreet word with Pietro.' He gestured in the direction of the restaurant's maître d', who immediately locked eyes with the detective and glided effortlessly among the tables towards him.

Sir Ernest and Lady Templeton watched with interest as the head waiter gave Fleming his ear. When Fleming had finished, without a word Pietro stood erect, bowed stiffly, and made a hasty retreat.

'What on earth was that all about?' asked Sir Ernest.

With a genial smile Fleming said, 'I wish to close the stable door, *before* the horse can bolt.'

'I see,' said Sir Ernest, although not seeing in the slightest.

Fleming returned to his dessert. 'You were saying, Lady Templeton, about your stay here in Venice?'

Her ladyship smiled warmly. 'We've just arrived.

We understand you're leaving the day after tomorrow, and... well, we hoped you might extend your stay? We'd like you to join us here in Venice a while longer.'

'I don't understand? Join you? In what capacity?'

'We'd like to hire you.'

CHAPTER THREE

THE STRANGER

Grand Hotel Venezia, Venice.

F leming made a small gesture to a waiter and a second bowl of *gelato* promptly arrived. 'Why would you require my services?'

Lady Templeton continued. 'Sir Ernest is an important man. I've heard stories of influential Englishmen being taken for ransom. Or murdered for political purposes. Your presence would put my mind at rest. I feel certain you could foresee and divert any potential danger.'

Fleming frowned. 'How long do you plan to stay in Venice?'

'Three weeks. We're at the Royale Fiore Hotel, a short distance from here. We leave for Constantinople at the end of the month.'

'I'm sorry, as much as I'd like to holiday further that would be quite impossible,' said Fleming. 'My work here is almost complete, and I plan to return to Avonbrook Cottage to rest, tend my roses, drink tea made in the way I like it. Oh, how I miss proper tea. I must also catch up on a growing pile of much neglected correspondence.'

'I told you,' said Sir Ernest. 'A man like Mr Fleming isn't going to be available at the drop of a hat.'

Lady Templeton became more insistent. She stiffened her posture. In the sparkling light of the chandeliers, her blonde hair looked almost white, her large blue eyes the colour of summer skies. 'On top of your usual fee, naturally, all additional expenses would be paid.'

'That's most kind but it's not about the money, Lady Templeton. I simply cannot, in all good conscience, stay on for three weeks without grounds upon which to do so. I'm needed back in England.'

'Mr Fleming's right. There really is no point...'

'There's also a bonus of twenty-five per cent of your usual fee at the end of the three weeks.'

Sir Ernest raised his thick dark eyebrows. 'Good lord, Carla! That's quite absurd.'

'Lady Templeton, my apologies. I see no reason for you to be concerned. From what you've told me, neither Sir Ernest, nor yourself, are in any imminent danger, and unless there's more behind your request, and most generous offer, then I respectfully suggest that you keep your money. There are a great many retired private detectives who could act as a chaperone should you so desire. Yes, my services are superior on many levels but my expertise is not what is required on this occasion. A man of modest capabilities will suffice.' Fleming frowned. In her eyes he could see there was something Lady Templeton had not told him. 'I sense there is more to your petition?'

Sir Ernest, an athletic-looking man with a square jaw and dimpled chin, puffed out his chest. 'This whole matter is stuff and nonsense! My darling wife exaggerates. I'm in no danger, I can assure you. Please explain to her, Fleming, that a peculiar visit from a stranger is quite normal for a man in my position and nothing to concern oneself with and, if anyone says otherwise they're talking poppycock! The world's full of crackpots.'

Fleming ceased eating, put down his silver spoon. His face grave, he fixed Sir Ernest with a steely look. 'There's more to this story of the stranger?'

Lady Templeton intervened. 'Yes, there is. There's one more thing. This was waiting for us when we arrived at the hotel.' She looked around surreptitiously, then reached into her beaded handbag and took out an envelope which she slipped discreetly into Fleming's hand. Sir Ernest and Lady Templeton watched as the great detective scrutinised the envelope, sniffed it and turned it over in his hands. Satisfied, he took out and unfolded the letter. His astonishment was apparent. 'There is nothing more?'

'That's exactly as we received it.'

The envelope contained a folded sheet of paper with a single word written upon it: MURDER. There was also a short piece of blue ribbon. He rubbed the ribbon between his fingers, then did the same with the sheet of paper which he also held up to the light to examine its grade and watermark. 'Have you received more of these communications?'

'No. This is the first.' Lady Templeton, feeling a sudden chill, took her husband's hand and turned to look around to see if they were being watched. 'What worries me most is that there's a connection between the visitor and this letter, that he's somehow discovered we've travelled to Venice and has followed us here. It would mean he knows our every move!'

'I don't wish to alarm you further, but that would seem to me to be a logical conclusion.'

'Tell him the other important part, Ernest.' She gave him an encouraging nudge.

Sir Ernest puffed and grumbled. 'The fellow had an accent; a rather unusual manner of speaking. It could have been Spanish, French, Russian, or

Portuguese… For all I know he could have been a Scot!' He threw up his hands in despair. 'I'm useless at this sort of thing!'

'Did this visitor have a name?'

'He called himself Professor Bonnard.'

'I know it's a lot to ask but we really need your assistance,' said Lady Templeton.

'What can be done?' asked Sir Ernest.

'I take these matters extremely seriously. You were correct to bring this to my attention.' Fleming examined the letter once more then returned it and the blue silk ribbon to the envelope. He clasped his hands. 'The word "Murder" is possibly a threat. As for the piece of blue silk, I can only assume it has some significance for the sender.' He looked at them both. 'Neither of you have any idea who sent this letter?'

Sir Ernest shook his head.

'Come now. Surely you must have some inkling?'

'We would tell you!' Lady Templeton exclaimed. 'It's putting us both under enormous pressure. Ernest's insomnia is worse than ever!'

Sir Ernest suddenly looked haggard. 'Listen here, Fleming. Whatever this is hanging over us,' he squeezed his wife's hand, 'is as much a puzzle to me as it is to you. If we knew who it was, we'd find some way to end it once and for all – but we don't! For pity's sake, we'd tell you, just to see the back of it. I can only assume I've inadvertently caused this lunatic some offence. All in all, Carla and I treat people fairly. We always have done.'

'This is something I've heard to be true,' said Fleming. 'If it were not, I can assure you, this meeting would have already ended.'

Fleming tapped his fingers rhythmically on the table and sighed. 'There's a lot about this that troubles me. It's my professional opinion that you should cancel your trip, and return at once with me to England.'

'I won't do it!' Sir Ernest blasted. 'I promised Carla this holiday and, by God, she'll have it!'

'Maybe, Mr Fleming's right?' said Lady Templeton.

Sir Ernest's face turned scarlet. 'It's to celebrate our silver wedding anniversary and it's been planned months in advance! It's a very special occasion. If there's one thing you should know about me, Fleming, it's that I change my plans for no man, and certainly not some coward who sends threats by post. All I need to know from you is whether you'll help. If you say no then fine, we'll shake hands as gentlemen and go our separate ways. No hard feelings. What I will *not* do is let any of this folly spoil this anniversary trip for my darling Carla.'

Lady Templeton looked adoringly at her husband. 'As stubborn as you are, I love you dearly.'

Sir Ernest squared his shoulders. 'I'm not the sentimental type, you know that, but I've said from the day we married I'd put you first. I may have failed in that promise on more than one occasion but you know you'll be forever in my heart.'

'Forever in my heart,' repeated Fleming softly. 'Those words hold great weight with me. They speak of true love both in this life and the next.'

'Then I implore you, Mr Fleming. Please take up our cause, I can't lose Ernest. His health has been of concern to me lately and I fear all this additional pressure might be too much for him. I can assure you, he won't back down; he's as stubborn as they come. Our time in Venice will continue with or without you.'

Fleming pondered for a few moments before replying. 'If you insist you won't cancel, which is my preferred course of action, then I see no choice but to extend my stay. I'm at your service until the matter's resolved. I'll book into the Royale Fiore Hotel first thing in the morning.'

Lady Templeton threw her arms around her husband. 'Oh, thank goodness, Ernest; he's agreed!'

'Please, dear, we're in public,' muttered Sir Ernest. 'Thank you, Mr Fleming. We will of course make all the necessary financial arrangements. We had hoped you'd agree to our proposal and have already taken the liberty of reserving you a room.'

'Excellent!' said Fleming.

At the back of the restaurant there was a sudden commotion. Several Italian police officers had surrounded the table where the two Russians sat. Seeing no way out they raised their hands in surrender. They were quickly searched, their weapons removed, handcuffed and led away.

Fleming's eyes turned to Countess Volkov who looked visibly shaken by the incident. Apparently aware of her close shave, she looked towards Fleming and offered a faint smile of acknowledgement. Fleming reciprocated with a subtle bow of his head.

'Was that your doing?' asked Sir Ernest.

'The countess is Russian, a rich widow, now living in exile here in Venice. Despite her age, she has a keen eye and she hired me to watch the two men she'd observed following her in recent days. I quickly established they were hired assassins who meant her ill. I decided somewhere public was the best place to bait my trap. Due to her concerns, the countess had taken to dining in her room for safety. I, therefore, made it known that she planned to dine in the hotel's restaurant this evening. Right on cue they showed up to seek an opportunity to carry out their dreadful deed. I asked Pietro to make a phone call on my behalf to a close acquaintance at the head of the *Carabinieri*.'

'All this unfolding around us while we dined and I had no clue!' declared Lady Templeton.

'There was little to be done. The trap had been set, all I had to do was wait for it to be sprung. I have little doubt these rats are well known and wanted for several criminal acts, here and abroad.' Fleming returned to his *gelato*. 'This dessert is an absolute triumph. I never cease to marvel that such perfection can be created from so little.' He held up a spoonful of the icy deliciousness. 'Perfect!'

CHAPTER FOUR

MAN IN THE MIRROR

Royale Fiore Hotel, Venice.

Signor Durante entered the sumptuous lobby of the Royale Fiore Hotel. The ancient building in the heart of 16th century Venice exuded opulence. Ornate chandeliers hung like vast, magnificent jewelled flowers over marble floors polished to a mirror finish, casting brilliant, crystal clear light onto the original frescos and stuccoes adorning the ceilings and walls. Turkish rugs and antique furniture added a further level of luxury fit for royalty.

'Welcome, Signor Durante,' said Signorina Lombardi, the reception manageress. 'If there's anything you require during your stay, I'll be happy to assist. Signor Rossi will take your luggage to your room. Please be so good as to follow him.' She handed Durante his room key.

'*Grazi*.' The Italian nodded, but said little, only explaining his lack of conversation by adding, 'It's been a tiring journey.'

'May I take your suitcase?' said Rossi, reaching for the small leather trunk.

Durante moved the case out of reach. 'Thank you, but I'll keep it with me.'

'As you wish, Signor Durante. Your room is on the second floor. The elevator is this way.' The young porter led the way and Durante followed. 'Have you travelled far?'

'I've come from Florence. I'm recently retired and I've always wanted to visit Venice, so here I am.'

'If there are any specific places you'd like to visit please let me know. I've lived in Venice my whole life.' Rossi chatted incessantly and Durante was relieved to reach his suite.

'Here we are, signor.' The young porter reached into his pocket. Realising it was empty he patted his other pockets.

'Is something wrong?'

'I appear to have misplaced my master key. I could have sworn it was right here in my pocket. I must have put it down somewhere. I hope I haven't lost it. I only started working here a few weeks ago.'

Durante handed the porter the room key given to him at reception.

The young porter smiled awkwardly, took the key and opened the door.

Durante looked around. The suite was palatial, far in excess of what he required. 'Is there anything more... modest?'

Rossi didn't seem to understand the question. 'There are twelve rooms and they're all occupied. The Royale Fiore is very popular with guests, we...'

'In that case, this will have to do.'

The porter opened the blue painted wooden shutters to reveal the view outside. He stepped onto the large balcony and turned to Durante. 'There's a stunning view of the canals from here. You can watch the gondolas as they pass.' Noting Durante's lack of enthusiasm he closed the doors. 'If everything's in order I'll leave you to rest.'

As the porter turned to leave, Durante handed him a tip. '*Molte grazie.*'

'Would you like me to recommend some lesser known places to visit, cafés, restaurants?'

Durante placed a hand on the door and began closing it. 'Thank you, but I'll find my way.'

Durante placed his trunk on the bed and unfastened the catch. Having retrieved a thick file and a notebook he went to the writing bureau, opened the deepest drawer, placed the items inside, before locking it and slipping the key into his wallet.

Exhausted from his journey he decided to take a bath. He'd then enjoy a cognac at the bar, before getting an early night. He looked at his haggard reflection in the ornate golden mirror. Tomorrow was his birthday and once again he'd be alone. However, in the morning he would breakfast like a king, on good coffee and pastries.

THE HOTEL'S long lounge bar was as sumptuous as the rest of the hotel. Exposed beams, delicately painted frescos, glittering chandeliers, plushly upholstered golden armchairs and a Venetian-style terrazzo floor. In the corner of the room a pianist played Chopin on a grand piano, its golden legs ornately carved.

'As I always say, if a Martini's good enough for Rockefeller, then it's good enough for me,' said Teddy Kelleher. He winked at Sir Ernest, and raised his third cocktail of the evening to his lips, before adding, 'You both look so young, you must tell me your secret. To me twenty-five years of marriage sounds like a lifetime.'

Elsie Kelleher gave her husband's arm a squeeze. 'Unless of course, you're married to the right woman.'

Smiling toothily she twirled a curl of her hair with a finger.

'Quite so,' said Teddy. He brought his wife's hand to his lips and kissed it.

'Marriage isn't for everyone,' said Lady Templeton, 'of that I'm certain. Get it wrong and I can imagine it being quite abominable. If you're lucky enough to get it right then it's a joy.'

'Here, here!' said Sir Ernest. 'It's my belief that the secret to staying young and fit is exercise, good food, and a happy wife!'

Elsie turned to Lady Templeton. 'Venice is your way of celebrating?'

Lady Templeton nodded, her large blue eyes widening with excitement. 'It was Ernest's idea. He suggested this anniversary trip as a special way to mark the occasion. I never actually thought it would happen. Yet, here we are!'

'It's such a fabulous idea.'

'They say this is among the finest hotels in Venice. From what I've seen so far, I'd tend to agree. The place is quite something,' said Teddy.

'The grandeur makes one feel quite at home,' remarked Lady Templeton. 'We have a country pile just south of London.'

'Is that so?' said Elsie. 'I can't abide the country myself. I'm a city girl through and through. I love the restaurants and theatres too much to leave. I even do some acting myself from time to time. It's only a bit of fun but I love it!'

Teddy waved his hand excitedly. 'You're here! This is Captain Jim Maitland, my best friend in the whole world.' He grabbed the captain around the shoulders and gave him a squeeze. 'He's joining Elsie and me on our little adventure. Quite reluctantly I might add. He prefers to keep his feet on dry land. Hated the boat trip, and claimed he'd rather fly. Can you imagine! Anyway, we're hoping to find him a beautiful heiress to make an honest man of him.'

Captain Maitland tucked his walking cane under his arm and shook hands with Sir Ernest. 'A pleasure to meet you. Please ignore Teddy, the man's a buffoon.'

Teddy guffawed.

Having noticed the limp and the cane, Sir Ernest's eyes glanced at Captain Maitland's leg.

'It's the result of a machine gun bullet. I was lucky,' explained Captain Maitland. 'By the grace of God I didn't lose it. It just means my rugby ambitions had to be shelved, permanently.'

Sir Ernest chuckled. 'That's the spirit. Always look on the bright side.'

Teddy slipped a hand around Elsie's waist. 'Like yourselves, Captain Maitland has never visited Venice before. I told him he didn't know what he was missing.' He nudged his friend with his knee. 'I intend to show you the highlights personally. It took Elsie to convince him he should join us. She can be most persuasive when she puts her mind to it.'

'There was really nothing to it,' said Elsie. 'I simply refused to let him continue moping around his flat. I ordered him to join us. I told him he had to come, and I wouldn't take no for an answer.'

'Captain Maitland, how do you and Teddy know each other?' asked Lady Templeton.

Teddy jumped in. 'He and I have been chums for years. We're practically brothers.'

'I'll admit, I feel perfectly sidelined at times,' said Elsie. 'They're more often than not off planning some boyish caper. It can be quite vexing.'

'That's complete tosh,' said Teddy. 'But a chap must have his fun. Where would we be if men couldn't shoot the occasional grouse or pheasant, take in a cricket match, race motorcars, or enjoy a spot fishing? We'd be in a right old pickle, that's where we'd be. Don't you agree, Sir Ernest?'

'If I were to be perfectly honest, I've never had much time for shooting or sport. I enjoy a round of golf and I certainly like to fish, that I will admit to.'

'When it comes to fishing I tend to agree with Sir Ernest. There's nothing more peaceful than sitting on a riverbank, early on a Sunday morning, alone with your thoughts, listening to the birds and the gurgle of the river while waiting for a fish to bite.'

'Captain Maitland, you make it sound so romantic,' said Lady Templeton.

'You're a helpless romantic, aren't you, Matty?' said Elsie. She pinched his cheek. 'And all the better for it.'

FERN BLAKE and Nancy Perkins peered into the hotel's bar. Nancy anxiously pressed her leather handbag to her side. The two modestly dressed English widows observed their fellow guests for a moment before venturing in. 'Shall we treat ourselves to a tipple, Nancy?' asked Fern.

Nancy nervously toyed with her pearl necklace. 'Yes, let's do that, Fern,' she murmured, her voice soft and timid. 'Just a small one, though. You know the drink goes straight to my head these days.' She stuck close to Fern as they moved to the bar.

'Just a small one it is,' agreed Fern. 'What would you like?'

'I don't rightly know.' Nancy ran her eyes over the array of bottles along the back of the bar, then up and down the swarthy bar man. When he smiled she felt her neck prickle.

Fern looked around at the small gathering in the middle of the room. 'What they've got looks nice.'

'It does, Fern. It does.' Nancy placed her crocodile leather handbag on the bar and, smiling sweetly, made herself comfortable on a stool. She pointed a gloved finger. 'Two of what they're having, please.'

The bartender gave a dignified nod. 'Two Martinis coming up.'

'Isn't this exciting, Fern? Look at all these moneyed gentlefolk.'

'We should introduce ourselves at the earliest opportunity,' suggested Fern.

'You're right. We should.' Nancy adjusted her greying hair which was pulled into a sedate bun and skewered in place with a silvery French pin.

They picked up their drinks and were about to head over when Signor Durante appeared and ordered a large cognac. He glanced at the women, and was about to introduce himself when his eyes fell upon a lone figure, sitting perfectly upright, at the side of the room.

Fern and Nancy's eyes followed his, wondering what had so instantly caught his attention.

Dressed in a perfectly tailored light grey suit, with high gloss, mahogany brown leather shoes, a man sat holding a newspaper and drinking tea, yet to Signor

Durante's keen eye it was clear he wasn't reading, but observing those gathered.

'You're Italian?' enquired Fern.

Signor Durante didn't immediately answer the question; his attention had turned to the group of five at the centre of the room. 'For my sins!' he said eventually, his face now breaking into a friendly smile. 'My apologies, I should introduce myself. I'm more than a little jaded from my recent travels.' He took each lady's hand in turn and kissed it. 'I am Antonio Durante. At your service.'

'Goodness me! At our service. How very continental. Are you here alone?' asked Nancy, suddenly feeling flustered and giggly.

'Sadly, yes. I'm holidaying by myself. I'm unmarried but always looking for the next Mrs Durante. My wife, she's no more.'

'That's dreadfully sad. I'm so sorry. A handsome man such as yourself, to be widowed in the prime of his life. How did she die? If you don't mind my asking.'

Durante nearly spilt his cognac. 'My apologies. She's not dead. My English is not as good as it could be. To me she is no more. We're divorced. She remarried a swine...'

Fern raised an incredulous eyebrow.

Durante searched for the right words 'No, not a

swine… a pig farmer. Yes, she married a farmer of pigs. She moved to Parma and is happy now. Me? I'm not so happy, but what can I do? He is an artisan while I… am not. He owns many hogs, and makes some of the finest hams in all of Italy. From time to time he will send me a parcel. I lose my woman but I gain the most exquisite *prosciutto di Parma*.' He pinched his thumb and fingers together and kissed them. '*Magnifico!*'

'Well I never,' said Nancy. 'How very peculiar. And what brings you to Venice?'

'Apart from your search for the next Mrs Durante,' added Fern playfully.

'I'm here to explore. I'm keen to absorb the history and experience the famous gondola on the Grand Canal.'

'Us too! Aren't we, Nancy? Your typical tourists, that's what we are. Here to embrace all Venice has to offer.'

'And more!' Nancy nodded enthusiastically. 'We can't wait to see all the places we've read about.' She produced a book called *The Heart of Venice*. 'I've read this from cover to cover more times than I care to mention.'

'She's not fibbing, you know. Loves to read does Nancy – when she's not knitting that is!'

The bar began to empty as guests moved to the dining room for dinner. 'Would you care to join us,

Signor Durante?' The Martini had emboldened Nancy.

He looked at the two women apologetically. 'I will forgo dinner this evening. Fatigue has got the better of me. However, I would be honoured to dine with you on another occasion. If that's agreeable?'

'That would be most delightful.'

'Sublime, Signor Durante,' agreed Fern. She enjoyed seeing her usually reserved friend flourish as she became comfortable with her surroundings.

Durante bid the two women good evening, and they left arm in arm, chatting excitedly. He stayed at the bar with his back to the room, nursing his cognac. Using the reflection in the huge ornate mirror behind the bar he watched each guest as they left for dinner. There was plenty of merriment and the only guest to notice his observing was the sharply dressed Englishman, whose newspaper was now folded on a small table beside the chair he'd vacated. He was certain he knew the man to be the private detective Henry Fleming. When their eyes met, briefly and unexpectedly, in the reflection of the mirror, Durante nodded politely. Fleming reciprocated. He did not stop or introduce himself, just followed closely behind the group of five.

CHAPTER FIVE

SWEET DESSERTS

The dining room hummed with conversation as the guests discussed the events of their day and introduced themselves to those recently arrived. The long dining table was dressed with pristine white damask, elegant floral arrangements and tall candles in silver holders spaced meticulously along its centre.

Fleming took his seat between a young Italian in his mid-twenties, who introduced himself as Gerardo Castelli, and Dr James Ingrey, a retired doctor.

'A private detective?' asked Gerardo politely. 'How extraordinary.' He was classically Italian in appearance. A darkly handsome, slim young man, with a long face, and an inquisitive glint in his brown eyes.

'What a jolly interesting coincidence,' said Dr Ingrey. 'I'm from your neck of the woods, Mr Fleming. For years I've been practising medicine in a quaint little village in Hampshire only a stone's throw from you in Dorset. You won't remember, I'm sure, but we met briefly once before. My brother is...'

'Cameron Ingrey,' said Fleming without hesitation. 'Your sister-in-law's brother murdered their uncle. The late Lord Randall.'

'Well I never!' exclaimed the doctor. 'You have a remarkable memory. That was nearly five years ago. A very sorry happening, indeed.'

'It was one of my first cases after returning from duty. I remember it well. How are your brother and sister-in-law?'

'They're as well as can be expected. My brother still struggles with his health; he's not been the same since returning from the Front.'

'I'm sorry to hear that. Please pass on my regards.'

'What brings you to Venice, Mr Fleming?'

It had been agreed that Fleming should not announce the truth behind his presence there. 'The sweet desserts,' he said with a smile. 'And a close second, the history and romance of one of the world's great cities. Yourself?'

'Much the same. I recently retired from full time practice. I keep my hand in of course, I wouldn't know what to do with myself if I gave up medicine completely. Also, with my Catholic upbringing, I've felt compelled to visit for many years. I thought I should do so before I got too old.'

The two men chuckled.

'How about you, Gerardo? Which part of Italy are you from?' asked Dr Ingrey.

'I've lived in various cities so I consider myself part Roman, part Florentine, part Sicilian, part... you get the idea.'

'And what brings you to Venice?'

'That's simple. I'm here for the music. In my heart I'm a musician and poet. I simply adore the opera. The more tragic the better.'

'I'm hoping to catch an opera myself while I'm here,' said Dr Ingrey.

'A night at the opera,' sighed Elsie Kelleher. She sat between Captain Maitland and her husband, across the table from Gerardo. 'What do you say, Teddy? Can we go?'

'Did somebody say opera?' asked Lady Templeton. She nudged Sir Ernest. 'We're hoping to go but we heard tickets are like gold dust.'

'I would be happy to arrange tickets for everyone, should it be of interest. A cousin of mine lives here in Venice, he will make seats available for as many as would like to go.'

'That's a splendid idea!' said Teddy. 'All of us together.'

'Oooh, Fern! How joyous. A night at the opera at last. Can you imagine?'

'I know, Nance! Just sublime. Dreamt about it, haven't we, dear?'

'It's settled. I'll make the arrangements,' announced Gerardo. He got to his feet and raised a glass. 'To new friends and new experiences!'

'New friends and new experiences!' repeated the guests.

Fleming raised his glass and thanked Gerardo. 'From where in Italy have you come?' he asked when Gerardo was once again seated.

'Genoa. It has a picturesque port, and the people are friendly and welcoming.'

'I know a little of Genoa. I have some interest in European history,' said Dr Ingrey. 'I believe Christopher Columbus was born there.'

'You're correct,' said Gerardo. 'Perhaps I get my love of travel from him. Who knows, he might be an ancestor of mine.'

'Wouldn't that be something?' the doctor chuckled.

Gerardo's attention was caught by the young woman sitting beside Lady Templeton. He turned to Fleming and looked at him questioningly. 'The young woman with Lady Templeton, is she her daughter?'

Fleming shook his head. 'She's Lady Templeton's companion, Miss Dolores Frost.'

'I see.' He was thoughtful for a moment. 'Lady Templeton has no children?'

'They had two sons. Edward and Arthur, both lost in the war. Miss Frost provides Lady Templeton with some *female* companionship.'

'Of course, I understand. Would it be acceptable to invite Miss Frost to the opera?'

'Perfectly acceptable.'

Gerardo smiled with pleasure. 'I think I would like to properly introduce myself to her, and Lady Templeton, tomorrow.' He appeared mesmerised by her short red hair.

Dr Ingrey chuckled and said discreetly to Fleming, 'I think the young Italian might have an interest in Miss Frost. It must be that the romance of Venice is already working its magic.'

'You might be right.'

The main course arrived along with more wine and champagne.

Mrs Elsie Kelleher searched her sequinned purse. 'I've left my lipstick in the room.' She turned to her husband. 'Teddy, would you be a darling and fetch it for me?'

Teddy was deep in conversation with Sir Ernest. 'I

wouldn't have a clue which one to get. Can't it wait? You look fabulous as you are.'

Elsie looked annoyed. 'Fine! I'll fetch it myself.' She stared at her husband.

'What?'

'Well, are you going to accompany me?'

Teddy looked frustrated. 'Sir Ernest is just telling me about his most recent round of golf at St Andrews, darling.'

Elsie's cheeks reddened. 'In that case, I'll go alone.' Her thick curly hair bounced as she turned away to hide her upset.

'I'll escort you. If you wish?' said Captain Maitland.

Teddy nodded. 'Yes, Matty will escort you. If it's imperative you have... whatever it is you said you needed. Good man.' He turned back to Sir Ernest. 'Sorry about that little interruption. You were saying about the seventeenth hole.'

Captain Maitland leaned on his walking stick as he pulled back her seat, and Elsie took his arm. The pair left the room. She came back, alone, thirty minutes later.

'Will Captain Maitland be returning?' asked Lady Templeton.

'He's taking a walk and having a smoke. He doesn't have much of an appetite.'

'I see,' said Lady Templeton. 'You're fortunate to have two such handsome men at your beck and call.'

Elsie put her hand on Teddy's arm and squeezed it lovingly. 'I suppose I am.'

Immediately the desserts were finished, Fern and Nancy excused themselves. 'We don't want to appear rude but it's been a long day and tomorrow we're hoping to get an early start. It's been a joyous evening.'

'What a pleasant couple,' said Dr Ingrey when they'd gone. 'They're quite the explorers and extremely well-travelled. A little quirky perhaps but, nevertheless, wonderful conversationalists. I wonder if they're sisters?'

'I look forward to making their acquaintance very soon,' said Fleming. He took his pocket watch from his waistcoat. 'It's getting late. I too shall retire shortly.'

'Still a man who prefers a pocket watch, I see,' remarked the doctor.

'I'm old-fashioned in that way. It also has considerable sentimental value.' He closed the case and tucked it away, gently patting it twice.

Seeing Miss Frost rise and leave the room, Fleming excused himself and followed her. He caught up with her in the hotel lobby.

'Good evening, Miss Frost,' said Fleming. 'Are you well?'

She frowned. 'Yes. Why?'

'Forgive me for saying but you seemed a little out of sorts this evening. You were unusually quiet at dinner. I don't know you well but on the occasions we've met you were very bubbly. Tonight, you hardly said two words to anyone.'

'I'm perfectly fine. I'm tired from all the travel, and the heat doesn't agree with me.'

From the dining room came Gerardo, Teddy and Dr Ingrey. They were laughing at a joke Teddy had made. Gerardo smiled winningly at Dolores.

Her cheeks flushed at the unexpected attention. 'Excuse me, Mr Fleming. I was on my way to my room. Good night.'

'Good night, Miss Frost.'

'Are you coming to the bar for a nightcap, Fleming?' hollered Teddy.

'Tonight, I must decline. Enjoy the rest of your evening, gentlemen. I'll see you in the morning.'

'Oh, come on!' After several further attempts to persuade him to change his mind, and failing, the three men continued to the bar, their conversation loud and boisterous.

Elsie appeared with Sir Ernest and Lady Templeton, and they took a lift together. Fleming was about to begin climbing the stairs when he noticed Captain Maitland sitting quietly on the hotel's terrace. He was drinking Scotch, and staring up into the night sky.

'Captain Maitland, I was hoping we might speak at dinner.'

'I'm sorry, Mr Fleming. There are times when I need to be alone. In those moments I don't make great company.'

'I understand. I shall bid you good night.'

'Before you go, Mr Fleming, there's something I could ask you. You're obviously a worldly man and I'd value your opinion.'

'You've intrigued me.'

Captain Maitland took a long sip of his drink, put down the glass and turned to Fleming. 'I've fallen in love.'

'You have?'

He nodded. His expression was grim. 'She's bright as a button, full of joy, with a beauty that stops my heart whenever I'm with her. Night and day I dream of making her mine.'

'I sense there's a problem?'

'There is.' His sigh was long and loud. He took out a silver cigarette case, offered one to Fleming, who refused, lit his cigarette, and having snapped the case closed placed it on the table.

'She's spoken for?' said Fleming.

Captain Maitland returned to staring at the stars. 'Yup.'

'Matters of the heart are not my field of expertise.

However, if it's possible to distance yourself from temptation then I would advise you do so.'

'Don't they say absence makes the heart grow fonder?'

'Only if you can't fill the void her absence has left with other distractions. As I said, I'm no expert.'

'Perhaps you're right, Fleming. In truth, I don't see what choice I have.'

'Your options are limited. The safest course of action is to find a way to move on. I know it's harder than it sounds but you must do what's right. Involving yourself with a married woman would be foolhardiness of the highest order.'

'You're right, of course. I don't know why I'm even considering it. I believe I simply needed to say it out loud. Thank you.'

'Good night, Captain Maitland.' Fleming turned to leave. 'Don't forget your cigarette case.' He pointed to the table.

'Ah, yes. I'm always misplacing it. I'm already losing my mind over a woman; I don't want to lose my cigarettes too. Imagine the state I'd be in then!' He chuckled to himself.

CHAPTER SIX

PROFESSOR BONNARD

On the terrace of the Royale Fiore the four of them sat at a shaded table, Fleming softly drumming his fingers on its smooth surface. He'd called them together to further understand events before their arrival in Venice. 'This is more serious than I had first understood it to be.'

Lady Templeton, Dolores and Sir Ernest nodded in agreement.

'I feel certain there's a connection,' said Lady Templeton.

'It would seem as though it's more than coincidence,' Fleming said gravely. 'Your home, Swallowbarn Hall, broken into and your diamond necklace stolen?'

'That's correct,' said Lady Templeton.

'It happened the day after the mysterious visitor,'

added Dolores. Her red hair, which fell just below her ears, was held back from her face with a thin silver band. Her usually pale white skin was pink from the sun across her forehead, nose and cheeks. 'Around lunchtime there was a knock at the front door and the stranger introduced himself as Professor Bonnard. He told me he had to speak with Sir Ernest. I asked him to wait in the drawing room, which is where he stayed until Sir Ernest arrived and showed him through to his study.'

'Describe Professor Bonnard to me.'

She hesitated. 'Well, without meaning to be rude, he was a funny-looking man with small round spectacles, long grey straggly hair, and face whiskers. He was dressed in a brown striped suit, brown shoes, and he wore brown leather gloves. I thought that was particularly odd because it was a cool day, but not cold enough for gloves.'

'Was there anything else that struck you as unusual about him?'

'His accent was strange. I couldn't make out where he was from.'

'Did you ask?'

'He was vague. I remember he told me he had lived in many countries throughout his life.'

'There is of course one other thing to consider.'

'What's that?' said Dolores.

'Professor Bonnard was in fact English and used an accent to hide his identity.'

'It's possible, I suppose.'

'You said "he", but could it have been a woman?' asked Fleming.

'Good heavens! I don't think so. Although it's true to say he kept his gaze down and his features were hidden behind glasses and a beard, but it would have had to have been a quite remarkable actress to carry it off.'

'The name *Bonnard* suggests the visitor could be French,' proposed Fleming.

'Possibly, but I'm not certain he sounded French. As I say, it was an odd way he spoke.'

'I only met him in passing,' explained Lady Templeton, 'but I certainly noticed the way he kept his answers short and wouldn't look me in the eye. I was busy and never really gave it much thought until after the break-in.'

Fleming turned to Sir Ernest. 'This Professor Bonnard, was his meeting with you scheduled?'

'On the contrary, he turned up out of the blue. I'd been planning to go into town and had to delay it.'

'The meeting itself, what did he want to discuss with you?'

Sir Ernest scratched his head, then gently smoothed his dark wavy hair with his hand. 'He told me he was staying in England for a while and that a friend of mine at the golf club had suggested he introduce himself. He was a friendly enough chap. He explained he'd be in town for a few days and hoped we'd have a chance to dine together and discuss a little business idea he had. He didn't elaborate on what that might be, but suggested it could be quite lucrative. I realise now, it was all nonsense. He was clearly casing the place.'

'Did you leave him alone at any point, Sir Ernest?'

'I really don't recall. It's possible.' He shook his head with frustration. 'The truth is I was rather unwell that day. I hadn't had much sleep, and I wasn't thinking clearly.'

'You've been unwell?'

'From time to time I find it hard to sleep. A long bout of this blasted insomnia makes it difficult to concentrate.'

'Insomnia is something Sir Ernest has struggled with our entire married life,' added Lady Templeton. 'We joke that perhaps marriage is the cause.' She chuckled lightly at their shared joke.

Sir Ernest kissed her hand. 'On the contrary, my love. Whatever the cause, I can assure you it has nothing to do with you.'

'I'm sorry to be asking so many questions but

could you tell me more about the necklace?' said Fleming.

'As I mentioned, it was my mother-in-law's and she gave it to me as a wedding gift. Three antique Russian diamonds. Quite lovely,' said Lady Templeton. 'And irreplaceable, of course.'

'It was clearly this Professor Bonnard,' said Sir Ernest. 'I asked around at the golf club and nobody had heard of the fellow. He'd fabricated the whole story in order to gain access to the house. You see, the necklace was kept in the safe in my study and it's obvious now that he was there to get a closer look.'

'You mentioned the diamonds during the meeting?'

'Well no, but I'm certain he was there to get a feel for the place. You know how these professionals operate better than I, Fleming.'

'I will admit I have some experience in such matters, I've apprehended thieves and recovered jewels in the past.' He turned to Dolores. 'You claimed to have seen this mysterious Professor Bonnard again?'

'I saw him the very next day. I rode my bicycle down to the stream. If the weather's nice I'll often sit beside the bridge and eat my lunch. It's a very pleasant spot. I was just finishing when I noticed a figure, quite some distance away, walking along the riverbank. At first I thought it must be one of the farm hands and was about to wave when I realised it was him, Professor Bonnard. I watched as he jumped across the stream and headed back towards town. He must have taken the old path from Swallowbarn Hall; it's an old shortcut between the house and church, somewhat overgrown now and rarely used. We take the motorcar to church along the new road these days.'

Lady Templeton patted her brow with a handkerchief. 'I also saw him. That evening, as the sun was going down, a devil-like figure was stalking through the wooded meadow. The way he moved, and skulked in the shadows, I could have sworn it was Professor Bonnard.'

'He'd obviously been snooping around,' said Sir Ernest. 'Because it was that night that the break-in occurred and the necklace was stolen.'

'I shall need the name of the detective handling the investigation.' Fleming pondered all he'd learned. 'As for the note you received upon arrival, I wondered whether anything's come to mind regarding the blue ribbon?'

They all shook their heads.

'We've talked about it and none of us can imagine what it means,' said Lady Templeton. 'Perhaps a practical joke?'

'If so, it's in very bad taste,' said Dolores.

'I can't believe it's connected to the theft of the

necklace. I've never heard of such a thing. It would be an odd type of thief who sends cryptic messages after a robbery,' suggested Sir Ernest.

'I'm not so sure, darling,' said Lady Templeton. 'Who's to say how the mind of a person like this Professor Bonnard works.'

'I quite agree,' said Fleming. 'We must keep an open mind and consider every alternative. It's only then will the answer to this most curious turn of events become clear.'

CHAPTER SEVEN

THE GRAND CANAL

Teddy Kelleher placed both hands on the edge of the reception desk and narrowed his eyes. 'Listen to me, carefully. My wife's brooch has been stolen.'

'You're quite sure, Signor Kelleher?' asked Signorina Lombardi, her expression of concern never wavering as she listened to his accusations.

'It was in our room. In her jewellery box. Now it's not. It's gone. Vanished.'

'Nothing else was stolen from the jewellery box, or the room?'

'Correct.'

'The thief ignored the other jewellery, the more valuable items, and stole only the brooch?'

He sighed. 'As I've said repeatedly: only the brooch was taken.'

'Yet the brooch was not valuable, Signor Kelleher?'

'Not particularly. As we established, there were other more valuable items but for some reason the thief left those behind.'

'This is most peculiar. Why would a thief not steal all the jewels?'

'How on earth would *I* know? Perhaps he was disturbed while in the act. Or he wasn't a particularly clever thief! I imagine there are competent thieves, and incompetent thieves. I'm quite certain there's no minimum qualification required to become one.'

Signorina Lombardi listened sympathetically.

'Before I call the *polizia*, are you certain the brooch hasn't been misplaced?'

'What? No!' Teddy threw his arms in the air. 'Aren't you listening to me? It's been stolen, nicked, pilfered, filched, pinched, whatever you want to call it – that's what's happened!'

Elsie and Captain Maitland, having finished a further search of the room, now arrived at reception.

'Well?' Teddy demanded.

'Nothing,' said Captain Maitland.

'It's most definitely been stolen.' Elsie was emphatic.

The reception manageress picked up the telephone, put a hand over the mouthpiece. 'This could take some time, Signor Kelleher.'

'It already has!' retorted Teddy sniffily. He ran a frustrated hand through his hair and turned to his wife. 'There's no point us all losing a day. Why don't you and Matty go? If this is resolved I'll join you later.'

'That seems rather unfair. It would be better if I stay behind,' said Captain Maitland. 'You and Elsie should spend the day together. I don't mind remaining here.'

'Not on your life, old man. You go. Look after Elsie. I'll stay here to make sure the theft is treated seriously.' He kissed Elsie on the cheek. 'Go!'

On the other side of the foyer stood the group that had booked to take a trip on the Grand Canal. Signor Durante had gone for a walk and was unsure whether he'd be joining the excursion. Fleming stood with Sir Ernest, Lady Templeton and Miss Frost. Nancy, Fern, Dr Ingrey and Gerardo discussed the theft of Elsie's brooch.

Sir Ernest whispered to Fleming, 'Should you take a look into this for them?'

'It's a matter for the local police. Your own plight is my only consideration at this time.'

In a low voice, Dr Ingrey aired his concerns to Gerardo. 'I do hope it turns up. It clearly has some important sentimental value.'

'If nothing else was taken, I find it hard to believe it actually *was* stolen,' said Gerardo.

'It probably came loose,' added Nancy helpfully. 'I lost my dear mother's brooch that way.'

'She did,' said Fern. 'Marcasite and pearls it was.'

The conversation hushed when Elsie and Captain Maitland joined them. Nancy shouldered her crocodile leather handbag, and gently squeezed Elsie's arm. 'I do hope it turns up, dear,' she said softly.

'Me too,' said Elsie. As the group began to move she turned to Teddy and blew him a kiss. He didn't notice. He was absorbed in a three-way conversation with the receptionist and the police officer on the end of the phone.

GONDOLAS LINED the Grand Canal near the Rialto Bridge for almost as far as the eye could see. They split into three groups and set off in separate boats along the historic waterway, the gondoliers, for the most part, keeping pace with one another.

Gerardo had made a point of speaking to Sir Ernest and Lady Templeton, which Fleming now felt certain had been a ruse to get closer to Miss Dolores Frost. He decided to allow Sir Ernest and Lady Templeton some space and with Gerardo and Dolores making a four, he joined Dr Ingrey, Fern and Nancy on the second gondola.

'Did you know, Miss Frost, that many of these buildings date back to the thirteenth century?' Gerardo ventured.

'Is that so?' she replied with a wry smile.

'And in fact the canal isn't really a river, it comes from a lagoon, connected to the Adriatic Sea, which means the direction and flow of the water changes with the tide.'

'Is that right?'

'Gondoliers are exclusively male. It's a prestigious role handed down from father to son.'

'Fascinating.' Dolores laughed. 'Are you going to keep this up all day?'

Gerardo looked taken aback. 'What do you mean?'

'You're clearly trying to impress me, Signor Castelli.' She raised her eyebrows, daring him to deny it.

He chuckled at the amused look on her face. 'Please call me Gerardo.'

'Then you must call me Dolores.'

His eyes fell on her scarred hand and arm, which she hurriedly hid.

'I'm sorry. I didn't mean to stare.'

'It's quite all right,' said Dolores. 'I'm used to it.'

'How did it happen?'

'Boiling water when I was a child. I pulled the pot onto me.' She ran a hand along her arm and side. 'My arm, side and hip got terribly scalded.'

'I'm sorry.'

'Don't be. There's no reason for you to concern yourself. I'm perfectly content and don't need sympathy.'

'I see that,' said Gerardo gently. 'You have fire about you. I like that.'

Dolores tried to hide her smile. 'Did you know the Rialto Bridge was originally a wooden draw-bridge which allowed ships with tall masts to pass? Having been damaged many times over the years it was eventually replaced with the stone bridge we see today.'

Gerardo laughed at Dolores's competitive spirit.

'Young love,' noted Dr Ingrey, gesturing towards Gerardo and Dolores in the other gondola.

'It would appear Lady Templeton doesn't approve of the budding romance.'

Dr Ingrey glanced at Lady Templeton whose gaze was fixed on Dolores. The young woman had her back to her ladyship and was unaware of the disapproval.

Despite a nervousness around water, Sir Ernest appeared to be a man transformed as he relaxed and took in the sights. He clutched his wife's hand. 'Do you see that, Carla?'

'What is it, Ernest?'

'Well, I'm not entirely sure, but it's quite a remark-able looking palace. Those columns and arches are exquisite. And can you see how the water comes right up to the front door?' He kissed his wife's hand.

'What was that for, my dear?'

'Insisting we come here, I suppose. All the pictures in the world cannot do it justice. It's also to, erm, say that, well, you're a jolly good wife. I might not always act like it, but I know I'm a lucky chap to have you.'

Lady Templeton chuckled. 'That was almost romantic, Ernest.'

'Was it? Good. Well then, happy anniversary, my dear.' He leaned over to kiss her cheek.

In the prow of the gondola, in front of Fleming and Dr Ingrey, Fern and Nancy sat huddled like pigeons on a garden wall. Chatting, and occasionally pointing out things of interest, the pair seemed uneasy at the jerking motion of the boat.

On the third gondola Captain Maitland sat with his injured leg out as straight as he could for comfort. Elsie sighed with contentment, transfixed by the beauty of Venice. Durante, who had decided he would join the excursion after all, sat behind them.

'I keep having to pinch myself to make sure this isn't a dream,' said Elsie. 'What do you make of it all, Signor Durante? How does Venice compare to Florence? That is where you're from, isn't it?'

'I'm not sure it's possible to compare one with the other. From the little I've seen of Venice so far it's certainly a fine city. However, for me, as a Florentine, my beloved Florence is the heartbeat of my world.'

'Very diplomatically put,' said Captain Maitland.

Durante declined an English cigarette offered by Captain Maitland preferring instead a French Gauloises.

'How long have you been married?' asked Durante. 'You make a fine couple.'

Captain Maitland's face reddened. Unsure what to say, he turned to Elsie.

Elsie giggled, her brown eyes shining mischievously. 'Matty and I aren't married. My husband, Teddy, is back at the hotel. He and the captain here are best friends and he's looking after me today. Aren't you, Captain?' She squeezed his arm fondly.

'My apologies. I'm embarrassed at my poor manners. I hope I didn't cause offence.'

'Not at all,' said Captain Maitland, forcing a smile.

'I'm a lucky girl. I have two extremely handsome and capable men taking care of me. What more could a woman want?' She swooped in and kissed Captain Maitland on the cheek.

Durante averted his eyes. 'Do you know any of the other English tourists?'

'We've only just met them all, but everyone seems jolly good company. It's fabulous we all get to experience Italy together,' said Elsie. 'I wish I'd had the opportunity to explore more of the world before settling down. I've wanted to see the Taj Mahal. Climb a mountain, and swim in tropical waters. Dip my toes in the sacred waters of The Ganges.' Elsie sighed.

'You can still do that,' insisted Captain Maitland. 'Teddy would grant you anything you wanted. You know that.'

'I know he would, but it's not the same. The adventures we have in our youth seem so much more... exhilarating. Life gets rather humdrum as we get older. I miss the passion of those days.'

'You're being silly, Elsie. You're still a young woman. There's plenty of time for adventures. You simply need to decide to make it happen,' said Captain Maitland.

'You're clearly a passionate and romantic woman,' said Durante. 'It might be that your ancestors were Italian, perhaps?' He smiled playfully.

'Wouldn't that be something, Matty?'

'Please don't go giving her ideas,' laughed Captain Maitland. 'You'll only encourage her.'

'Don't be like that, Matty, you sound grumpy like Teddy. And I adore that you're an optimist.'

'I'm hardly that. I might have been at one time, but not any more.' He rubbed his aching knee.

'Don't be absurd, of course you are. You bring a

smile to my face every time we're together. If ever I feel down you cheer me up, and if I have a problem you'll find an obvious solution. You're so practical. It's adorable. He's ridiculously self-effacing, Signor Durante. I've never known anyone like it.'

Captain Maitland loosened his collar. 'Perhaps.'

'There's no perhaps about it.' Elsie turned to Durante, her rich brown eyes narrowed. 'Do you dance, Signor Durante?'

Captain Maitland and Durante frowned with surprise at the abrupt change of topic.

'It's not something I've ever felt compelled to do.'

'Teddy refuses to dance and for obvious reasons Matty's incapable, but I'd love to dance under the stars by the light of a Venetian moon. Oh, doesn't that sound so wonderfully romantic!' She quivered with excitement.

'I'm sure it could be arranged.'

Durante could see sorrow in Captain Maitland's eyes as he shifted his leg for comfort.

When the gondolas returned to their stations, Gerardo alighted first then, having braced himself, extended a hand to assist Dolores. She hesitated before putting out her scarred hand. With a little jump and a giggle she landed safely. He then helped Lady Templeton. Sir Ernest stepped forward. Having decided he needed no help from the handsome Italian, he misplaced his foot and lost his balance. With lightning speed Gerardo grabbed him and kept him upright.

'I've got you,' said Gerardo, holding Sir Ernest's arm in a vice-like grip as he steadied him.

'Are you all right, Sir Ernest?' asked Fleming as he disembarked from his own gondola.

'Blasted vessels are a law unto themselves. The way they shift underfoot it's like standing on ice,' he fumed. 'Fortunately, Gerardo kept me from going head-first into the soup. I'll be buying you a drink, sir. Of that you can be certain!'

Gerardo smiled politely. 'If you insist.'

'It's the least I can do. Let's get as far from these death traps as possible. I'm famished.'

CHAPTER EIGHT

A SPOT OF BOTHER

After a satisfying lunch most of the group returned to the hotel to avoid the worst of the heat and seize the opportunity for a rejuvenating nap. By early evening, the sun's intensity had waned and the temperature was rather more agreeable.

Fern and Nancy walked arm in arm with Dolores whom they had accompanied on a visit to a nearby Gothic-Renaissance church she had heard was remarkable.

'Nancy and I might as well have been twins,' said Fern, cheerfully twirling her parasol.

'She's right,' said Nancy. 'We were born a few months apart. Different mothers just across the street from one another. Inseparable from the day we met, weren't we, Fern?'

She nodded. 'From the day we met.'

Dolores smiled from beneath her large sun hat. Her face had reddened further during the gondola ride along the Grand Canal and she was now taking more care to avoid her fair skin burning. 'I'm sure you have plenty of tales to tell.'

'Life was tough back then. There was work to be done, hard work, even for us young 'uns.'

'We found time to play when we could though, didn't we?'

The two women smiled. 'Yes, we did. I lost track of the number of times my mother had to fetch me from her back yard,' said Fern. 'Gave me a clip round the ear on more than one occasion, she did, I can tell you.'

'We've always been little monkeys, us two.'

'Up to no good back then and just the same today.' The two women cackled, their eyes sparkling.

'Good for you,' said Dolores. 'Though, two sweet ladies such as yourselves can't get into too much trouble, I'm sure.'

'Your generation's very lucky. You get away with things we never would have.'

'We'd certainly have given it a go though, that's for sure.'

'Yes, we would. How times have changed.'

'I'm a little behind the times,' said Dolores. 'All the parties, music, and drinking isn't really my scene. I find happiness in a good book and a cup of hot chocolate.'

Nancy patted her hand fondly. 'If that's what makes you happy, dear, who are we, or anyone, to disagree.'

'I will say one thing though,' said Fern. 'I'm certain the men are more handsome now than in our day!'

The three women giggled.

'You're right, of course,' said Nancy. 'Take that young Italian beau of yours. If I were thirty years younger...'

'Thirty years?' scoffed Fern. 'And the rest!' She playfully nudged her friend.

'Oi, you! Don't be so cheeky.'

Dolores frowned. 'I have no interest in Gerardo, or any man for that matter. He's pleasant company, but nothing more. Undoubtedly, he's handsome, and that might catch the attention of some women, but he doesn't interest me in the slightest, of that I can assure you.'

'I see,' Nancy ventured uncertainly.

'Is that so?' said Fern. 'Our apologies. We jumped to the wrong conclusion.'

'You certainly did,' said Dolores indignantly.

They walked in silence for a little while, though the unease didn't last long; the innocent charm of the two old ladies soon softened Dolores.

The three women turned into a narrow side street lined with busy boutique stores selling all manner of foods, glassware, jewellery, Venetian linen, and pottery, ornately decorated Carnevale masks, and leather goods.

Fern picked up a small, exquisitely painted vase. Turning it in her hands, she examined it then passed it to Nancy who, feeling the proprietor's beady eye fall on her, carefully put it down again. Keen to negotiate a sale, the shopkeeper approached, nodding enthusiastically and flapping her arms, as she talked price.

The women turned away, slowly moving from stall to shop to stall.

After an hour, as Dolores and Fern were admiring the quality of the lace outside what appeared to be a makeshift stall in front of the seller's home, out of nowhere came angry shouts and a furious shopkeeper appeared in front of them. Fern spun around looking for Nancy and was relieved to spot her sitting on a step in the shade. Blissfully unaware of what was about to unfold, she was reading her book and making notes in the margins.

Fern recognised the angry woman as the proprietor of a silverware boutique they had visited earlier.

Dolores, the focus of the woman's anger, was completely bemused. From the gestures she was making towards her wrist, it seemed it had something to do with a silver bracelet. The woman grabbed Dolores by the arm and tried to snatch her handbag.

'How dare you?!' shouted a struggling Dolores. 'It's mine!'

As a crowd began to gather, the silverware seller was joined by her assistant and two neighbouring shop-keepers. The woman shouted angrily, still desperately trying to seize Dolores's beaded bag.

'What's going on? Let go!' demanded Fern, slap-ping at the hands attempting to part Dolores from her handbag.

'Leave her alone!' A protective Nancy had now jumped to her feet and joined the fray.

Finally, the shopkeeper let go, but the three women were surrounded.

A skinny young man stepped forward, his wide mouth and thin lips giving him a reptilian look. Though his English was good, his accent made it diffi-cult to understand as he spoke so quickly.

'We must look inside.' He gestured abruptly at the handbag.

Dolores clutched the bag to her chest. 'Nobody's opening my handbag. How dare you!'

The young man pointed at the shopkeeper whose hair, piled high on top of her head, resembled a large grenade. It trembled as though it might explode at any moment. Her leathery, deeply furrowed face was pinched into a scowl.

'If you do not she will not let you leave. She says you steal from her. You understand? Steal?'

It was quite apparent they were in a Mexican standoff.

Nancy placed a comforting hand on Dolores's arm.

Fern sighed and turned to Dolores. 'Show her. Prove she's wrong. Otherwise they might call the police. None of us want that.'

'I heard they do this to make you buy something,' said Nancy.

Dolores began to cry. 'I don't want to cause any trouble.'

'I know you don't,' said Fern. 'Open your bag and then we can leave.'

Dolores nodded. She stepped towards the young man and snapped open her handbag. The shopkeeper leapt forward and snatched it from Dolores's grasp. She immediately rifled through it, her hand moving in a furious digging motion. After a few seconds of rummaging she looked confused, glaring first at Dolores and then the young man. She threw the bag to the ground and proceeded to pat Dolores down looking for pockets, but found none. Unhappy, but having to be satisfied, she turned and stormed off.

'Can we go?' asked Dolores tremulously, retrieving her bag.

The young man nodded.

'Not even an apology,' snapped Fern. 'You're accused of who knows what, publicly humiliated, and... the embarrassment!' She waved a hand at the crowd that had gathered. 'Get out of our way. How rude and indecorous. You should all be ashamed.'

Nancy wrapped an arm around Dolores and with Fern leading the way they headed back to the security of the hotel.

'I SIMPLY COULDN'T BELIEVE it. The shopkeeper just snatched my handbag from me!' said Dolores indignantly. Her slender, pale hands trembled as she sipped sweet tea, the scars making her look more fragile than ever. She tucked a wayward lock of red hair behind her ear.

'I should have insisted on coming with you,' said Lady Templeton. 'You poor, poor girl.'

'Did I mention how fearsome-looking the woman was? Quite monstrous. I'm sure I shall have nightmares.'

Fleming passed Dolores a china plate piled with *Torcetti*. 'Where are Fern and Nancy now?'

'They're resting in their room. Quite overcome with shock, I'm sure. It was wonderful, the way they stood up for me. You should have seen Nancy! Transformed from a timid kitten to a raging tiger.'

'It was certainly a blessing they were with you,' said Fleming. 'I'll speak to them later to ensure their time in Venice isn't spoiled by what is, no doubt, an unfortunate misunderstanding.' He smiled sympathetically. 'Though it's exciting to explore new places, my advice to you is that you don't venture too far without a male chaperone such as myself, Lord Ernest, or Captain Maitland. Any of us would be only too pleased to accompany you. As you've experienced today, there are differences between the familiar streets of home, and those of Venice.'

'An Italian prison cell is no place for so fair and delicate a young lady,' added Lady Templeton.

'I can stand up for myself when I need to,' insisted Dolores. 'It was just all so sudden and unexpected.'

'You're a very capable and independent woman, of that I've no doubt,' said Fleming. 'However, there is harm to be had even for the most worldly among us.'

Lady Templeton took Dolores's hand, holding it between her own. 'Promise me, you'll be more careful. My heart's beating at a tremendous rate, just hearing about it all. I should have insisted Lord Ernest went with you instead of snoring the afternoon away. Why don't you take some rest before dinner? You look quite drained.'

'I'll try but my head's spinning from all the excitement,' said Dolores.

When Dolores had left them, Lady Templeton turned to Fleming. 'What do you make of it all?'

'It's hard to say. I'm relieved the fracas didn't escalate further. The authorities in Italy work differently to those in England and naturally they don't take kindly to British interference.'

'You have contacts here?'

'This is true but there is only so much they can do.' Fleming raised a hand. 'Let's not entertain *what-ifs*. All is well. Dolores is safe, and a little wiser. A lesson learned, perhaps?'

'She's a sweet young woman and I feel lucky to have her as a companion. She keeps me feeling young and in touch with modern thinking.'

'A sharp and curious mind is a blessing one should never take for granted. It's as important as a healthy body. Talking of which, I should take a brief walk before dinner. I'll take the opportunity before Sir Ernest rises.'

'I presume, despite the threatening letter, you feel he's in no immediate danger? I suppose what I'm really asking is whether you have any concerns to share with me?'

'I've witnessed nothing to alarm me. You continue to lock the door of your room as instructed?'

'Day and night.'

'Perfect. You can rest assured, I'm staying vigilant and alert to every eventuality. If there's nothing else, Lady Templeton, I insist you continue to enjoy your anniversary holiday, and leave everything else to me.' He smiled reassuringly.

She nodded. 'Of course. I'm most grateful to you.'

'My pleasure.' They rose and Fleming watched as Lady Templeton returned to her room in search of Sir Ernest. He then picked up his hat and headed to the street for a short restorative stroll.

CHAPTER NINE

ITALIAN PASSIONS

U nder the shade of an awning, with a cool breeze off the Grand Canal being channelled between the narrow waterways and side streets, the doctor sipped his espresso. He screwed up his face. It was strong and bitter, not really what he'd expected at all. On arrival he'd looked around the coffee shop, and noticing the beverage was clearly very popular with the locals he'd thought *when in Rome*!

He wondered if, given time, he might eventually acquire the taste. However, he doubted it would ever replace his love of a good, strong, sweet cup of tea.

The doctor was about to catch the waiter's attention and request something more refreshing when who should appear but Henry Fleming. He raised a hand in greeting.

'You've caught me red-handed!' said Dr Ingrey.

'I'm supposed to be sightseeing but I don't seem to be able to go for more than an hour without needing some respite from this blasted heat. Day and night, it's almost intolerable! Can I get you something to drink?'

'That would be most welcome,' said Fleming. He removed his hat and sat down opposite the doctor.

With a wide smile the waiter placed two iced lemon waters on the table.

'There was a time when I swore I'd never leave England. Now, older and wiser, I feel a need to explore. Until this trip, my knowledge of the world beyond Britain has been gained from books. I even spent the war attending to patients at a series of military hospitals in and around Hampshire and Dorset. I presume your work means you're well-travelled, Mr Fleming?'

'I've been fortunate enough to see a good many countries, though not as many as I'd like. Travelling can be arduous and uncomfortable at times but the wonders one encounters, along with the memories and acquaintances made, somehow make the effort worthwhile.'

The doctor looked serious for a moment. 'I hope you don't mind my mentioning it but I heard you were here on a case.'

Fleming assumed the doctor was not referring to his arrangement with Sir Ernest and Lady Templeton as there had been an agreement to keep that between themselves. 'My investigation on behalf of Countess Volkov is concluded. I'm now here to enjoy a few days' rest. Why do you ask?'

'No reason. Simply good old-fashioned curiosity. Being a doctor for so many years I'm in the habit of asking questions. It helps to be nosy, I suppose.' He sipped his iced drink.

'In that we have something in common, Doctor. Questions are my stock-in-trade. However, I'd prefer we exchange "It helps to be nosy" with: it helps to have an inquiring mind!'

The two men chuckled.

'At our first dinner, I noticed you and Sir Ernest having quite an in-depth conversation. Would I be correct in thinking you had differing opinions on something?'

The doctor thought for a moment.

'Oh yes! I mentioned that he might have known a dear friend of mine, Lord Rossendale.'

'Lord Rossendale, the high court judge?'

'That's the fellow. Anyway, I was under the impression ol' Rosser and Sir Ernest had been good friends at one time.'

'And had they?'

'That's the odd thing. At the mention of Lord Rossendale's name Sir Ernest became agitated. From what I could ascertain they'd had quite the falling-out. They haven't spoken in decades.'

'Did he tell you why?'

'He didn't and it seemed rude to press the matter. It was quite plain to see he disliked the man.'

'Of course,' said Fleming.

The doctor's attention turned to something going on over Fleming's shoulder.

Fleming twisted in his seat and looked behind him.

'How peculiar,' said Dr Ingrey. 'Isn't that Signor Durante and Gerardo Castelli? They appear to be arguing. Looks quite heated too.'

At the end of the narrow street, which opened into a courtyard with a fountain at its centre, the two men could clearly be seen. Despite being unable to hear what was being said, there was no doubt they were in the middle of a dreadful disagreement. Durante had Gerardo by the arm of his jacket, his grip unrelenting as he restrained him. Gerardo pushed back and slapped Durante's hand away.

At that moment, a couple of lovers walked in front of Fleming and Dr Ingrey. The pair stopped and began to kiss. The young man smoothed the young woman's hair and tucked it behind her ear. He put his arm around her and they continued walking. By the time they moved on, Durante and Gerardo were gone.

'Well, Durante and Gerardo certainly seem to have fallen out,' said the doctor. 'What did you make of it?'

Fleming looked concerned but seeing the doctor observing him, quickly dismissed the incident. 'This heat encourages short tempers.' He took out his pocket watch. 'I should be getting back to the hotel.'

'I'll stay a while. There's a statue around here somewhere that I've heard is quite a work of art. I also enjoy admiring the street artists' work.'

Fleming thanked the doctor then at a quick march headed in the direction of the courtyard.

THE DINING ROOM was filled with the smell of freshly baked bread, pickled vegetables, and the rich aroma of tomatoes and basil.

Durante, who appeared unaware he'd been seen in the courtyard, was more talkative than usual and had joked several times with Fern and Nancy, his surprisingly dry wit making them laugh uncontrollably on more than one occasion.

Conspicuously absent from the table was Gerardo. His dinner place remained set but he'd not yet made an appearance. When questioned, neither Fleming nor Dr Ingrey mentioned the dispute they'd witnessed, and the speculation was that he was either under the weather or out sightseeing.

'What do you say, Mr Fleming?' asked Elsie Kelleher. 'We're having a little wager. It's nothing but a little fun.'

All eyes turned to Fleming.

'I'm uncertain of your question,' admitted Fleming.

'It's a riddle. I wonder what your answer might be?' She giggled excitedly. 'You walk into a darkened and ice cold room that contains a kerosene lamp, a fireplace, a match, and a candle. What would you light first?'

'I'd certainly light the kerosene lamp first,' said Teddy. 'Then I'd be able to see what I'm doing! Getting a fireplace lit in a darkened room is quite difficult to say the least.'

'Quite so,' Sir Ernest agreed. 'Either the candle or the lamp. It's obvious,' he puffed.

Fleming played along, pretending it was a taxing problem for him. Elsie's eyes shone with delight as she imagined she had the great detective stumped. 'You almost had me there for a moment, but I believe the answer is quite simple. The first thing you would need to light is the—'

'Match,' interjected Durante. 'You'd need to light

79

the match before you could light either the lamp, candle, or fireplace.'

The room erupted with laughter.

'How about that? He beat the great detective to it,' said Fern quietly to Nancy.

'Of course!' exclaimed Teddy, slapping his forehead.

'It was a trick question,' complained Sir Ernest. 'Obviously, you'd need to start with the match...'

Lady Templeton patted her husband's hand. 'Don't get uptight. It's just a bit of harmless fun.'

'It's rather silly, if you ask me,' he muttered under his breath.

'Bravo,' said Fleming, politely applauding Durante.

Elsie attempted to turn her attention to Captain Maitland with her next riddle. He wasn't having any of it and excused himself for a cigarette before the arrival of dessert and coffee. Others joined him.

'Please accept my apologies,' said Durante to Fleming. 'To steal your thunder in that way was childish of me.'

'There's nothing to forgive. Your timing was perfect and very entertaining for the other guests.' Seeing an empty seat beside Durante, Fleming moved closer. 'I understand you come from Florence?'

'It's the city in which I was born and I've spent my whole life there. I can't imagine living anywhere else.'

'Do you have family there?'

'My father grows tomatoes and basil on his balcony and complains about his neighbours making too much noise. My mother passed away several years ago. I have a sister who moved to Naples to marry a plumber, whom I know to be a womaniser. She didn't thank me for telling her the truth about him. They have twin girls. Nieces whom I adore. I have no children of my own. An ex-wife who I regret taking for granted.' He shrugged and laughed. 'It could be worse. I'm not sure how, but I'm certain it could.'

Fleming smiled. 'Your line of work?'

Durante hesitated.

Fleming studied him closely.

'I worked in construction for many years. The only good thing about it is that it's well paid.'

Durante jumped with fright when at the other end of the table Teddy knocked over a wine glass and it smashed on the stone tiled floor. Red wine had spilled onto Sir Ernest's trousers, which he now dabbed with his napkin.

'Are you okay?' asked Fleming. 'You seem a little on edge.'

'Of course. Why shouldn't I be? I have a lot on my mind at the moment. It's nothing. I have a heart condition. Most likely brought on by a lifetime of worry.'

'I'm sorry to hear that.'

'I take medication each morning. It's under control. My health is another reason I'm here in Venice. Under doctor's orders, I'm learning to relax and take life a little easier.'

'It's important to stop and smell the roses.'

Durante nodded. 'There's much truth in that.'

'I was surprised Gerardo missed dinner this evening. I believe you and he are close. I understand you were acquainted before your arrival here in Venice.'

Again Durante appeared thrown by the question. 'My English is a...' He waved a hand in the air as though he didn't quite understand.

Fleming had little doubt he understood perfectly. He repeated it anyway. 'Your friend, and fellow countryman Gerardo missed dinner. I'd been hoping to talk to him. He seems a very interesting young man.'

'I'm no more his friend than you are, Signor Fleming. He and I have never met before. Whoever told you he and I were acquainted was mistaken.'

'Nobody told me. It was merely down to observation. Clcarly, I'm wrong on this occasion. I also heard you and he had an angry exchange.'

'It would appear there are eyes and ears everywhere,' said Durante. 'I questioned his motives for arranging a trip to the opera for everyone. I wondered why he would do something so grand for a group of people he hardly knows. I suggested he was trying to impress Miss Frost and that he was foolish to be so reckless with his money.'

'He took offence?'

'It was stupid of me. I'm not used to such generosity from strangers, so I questioned it. It was nothing.'

'You grabbed him and raised your voice.'

Durante fixed Fleming with a searching look, trying to fathom whether it was in fact Fleming who had seen them. He said nothing for a long moment. 'To an Englishman it might have looked like more than it actually was. There are many cultural differences between our two great nations, not least of which is our passion. We Italians are known for it.'

'I wondered if it was the real reason Gerardo didn't appear for dinner.'

'You know, I'm going to skip dessert. It's a lovely evening. I think I'll find a nice little bar and have a drink or two. Good night, Signor Fleming.' With that Durante got to his feet and left the room.

'Is everything all right, Mr Fleming?' asked Lady Templeton from down the table.

'Yes,' smiled Fleming reassuringly. 'Perfectly fine.'

CHAPTER TEN

HIS STRONG EMBRACE

Elegantly dressed for the evening, Gerardo Castelli put out a hand to steady Dolores as they climbed the steps to the opera house. She acknowledged the gesture but with a polite smile refused it. 'I'm fine, thank you, Gerardo.'

'Of course,' he said. He turned to Lady Templeton who had dressed in a flowing gown of midnight-blue satin, purchased especially for the occasion. Her blonde hair had been coiled into the nape of her neck and was held in place by an elaborate comb of peacock feathers. Her face glowed in the warm evening light, her lovely blue eyes filled with anticipation.

'I'm not sure how I can ever thank you, Gerardo. You have no idea how exciting this is for me,' said Lady Templeton. 'Rigoletto is one of my all-time favourite operas.'

'It's my pleasure.'

'Absolutely, I couldn't agree more with my beloved. We're most grateful. I can't say I know what to expect, plenty of warbling and bellowing, I suspect. However, you never know; I might surprise myself and enjoy it.' Sir Ernest smiled appreciatively.

With everyone accounted for, they entered the opera house where Gerardo spoke privately to a uniformed member of staff who had miraculously managed to find them places.

'He's a cousin on my uncle's side,' explained Gerardo. 'The seats are not the finest but they are very good. We'll be comfortable.'

The orchestra was warming up as they were escorted down the aisle to their row. Gerardo thanked his cousin, who smiled and placed a white gloved hand on his heart, as he gave a slight bow before leaving.

When everyone was settled, Gerardo took the last remaining seat in the row. He watched as Henry Fleming adjusted his waistcoat and straightened his trouser creases, then carefully and gently folded his jacket, placing his hat on top. Finally, he checked his tie and cufflinks.

'There we are, that's better,' said Fleming to himself when he was comfortable.

'You could have left your things in the cloakroom, Signor Fleming,' said Gerardo.

Fleming leaned close to confide. He spoke as quietly as he could amid the surrounding hubbub. 'I avoid a public cloakroom at all cost. I'm not suggesting there's any deliberate act of dishonesty, only that items of importance may on occasion be *misplaced*, if you catch my meaning.' He gave a knowing wink.

'I can't imagine for one moment anything would go missing from a cloakroom here at *Teatro La Fenice*.'

'I'm sure you're right,' agreed Fleming. 'But I'm a creature of habit.' He coughed lightly to clear his throat and glanced along the row to where Durante was seated. 'I couldn't help but notice that there's some unease between yourself and fellow guest Signor Durante. Is everything all right between you?'

Gerardo huffed with exasperation. 'The man's a fool. We don't see eye to eye. Never will.'

'We cannot agree with everyone we meet.'

'That's the truth.'

'Was it any particular view upon which you found yourselves at loggerheads?'

The young Italian shook his head. 'We're different generations. He's very stuck in his ways and rather opinionated. He told me my interest in Dolores was inappropriate. That I should be pursuing a nice traditional Italian girl. I told him it was none of his business. I added that in fact Dolores had rebutted my interest, so he had nothing to worry about.' He looked

Dolores's way. She was deep in conversation with Lady Templeton. The two women were admiring the sculptures and carvings around the ceiling, and pointing to the enormous chandeliers which were themselves works of art.

'Your English is very good,' said Fleming.

'At a young age I was encouraged to learn English.'

'By your parents?'

He was about to continue when the lights dimmed. The audience fell silent. The anticipation that something spectacular was about to happen was palpable. There was applause as the conductor appeared. He took his place and raised his arms. Seconds later the orchestra struck up and the performance began.

'I'M NOT ENTIRELY sure what was happening for the most part, but I think I enjoyed it,' said Sir Ernest back at the hotel bar. He'd treated himself to a cigar and a large Scotch for having endured nearly three hours of utter confusion.

Lady Templeton shook her head and squeezed his arm. She gave him a peck on the cheek. 'It's late and I'm going to bed. Don't stay up too long.'

'I'll finish this cigar and possibly one more Scotch

and then I'll be along. Goodnight, my sweet.' He watched his wife as she said her goodnights to the other guests and left the room.

'You two are adorable,' said Elsie. She leaned on Teddy who was getting more drinks. 'I hope Teddy and I are as in love when we celebrate our twenty-fifth.'

Sir Ernest puffed a huge cloud of smoke into the room. 'From the day we met I knew she was the one. Since then I've only had eyes for her.'

'It was love at first sight?'

'I suppose it was.' He chuckled.

'It sounds so romantic.'

'I'm not sure she felt the same way. I had to do a bit of chasing but eventually she came around.'

'Do you hear that, Teddy? It was love at first sight.'

Teddy passed Elsie her Martini. 'Sounds great,' he said with uninterest. He looked around for the doctor. 'I'm going to have a chat with Dr Ingrey and Matty over there. All this talk of love at first sight, and romantic displays, on top of a night at the opera has me feeling quite out of sorts!'

Sir Ernest appeared uncomfortable being left alone with Elsie at the bar and soon made his excuses. He took his drink out onto the terrace to sit alone.

Elsie joined Dolores, Nancy and Fern who despite the late hour were still chatting excitedly. Nancy, reading glasses perched at the end of her nose, was knitting and listening, joining in from time to time. Fern sipped a hot chocolate.

Dolores was a little tipsy and stumbled over her words. 'Why does everyone think it's their job to find me a husband? I'm quite content without a man in my life,' she pouted. It was clear she felt rankled. She folded her arms, out of habit adjusting her sleeve to cover the scars.

'Nobody's trying to marry you off, my dear, we're just teasing. You have to admit, he's a fine figure of a man.'

Her eyes wide with interest Elsie said, 'Who's a fine figure of a man? Who are we talking about?'

'Why Captain Maitland of course,' said Nancy innocently without looking up from her knitting. 'The thought of his strong embrace makes me quite giddy.'

Dolores let out an undignified snort of laughter. Her red curls bounced as she threw back her head.

'Enough of that talk! It's entirely inappropriate,' said Elsie sharply.

'If you say so, dear,' agreed Fern equably. 'Though, I happen to agree with Nancy. You know the captain well, Elsie; does he have his eye on anyone? I might be old enough to be his mother but if Dolores isn't interested then I suppose that leaves the field clear for me.'

Elsie frowned when the three women laughed uproariously.

'Oh my goodness,' said Dolores breathlessly, dabbing at her eyes. 'You know something, Fern and Nancy? I don't think I've ever met anyone quite like you two before. You're completely outrageous.'

Elsie's face had flushed. She touched her curly hair, tucking it behind her ear. 'Well, I agree with Dolores. You shouldn't talk about Captain Maitland, or any man for that matter, behind their back in this way. It's... vulgar.'

This provoked even louder laughter.

Nancy peered over her reading glasses. 'You're quite... shall we say *protective* of Captain Maitland, aren't you, Elsie?'

'What's *that* supposed to mean?'

Fern and Dolores watched this exchange with interest.

Nancy lay her knitting down in her lap. She sucked her teeth. 'It's not my place to point it out, *Mrs Kelleher*, but if you can't see it you must be blind. Or perhaps you do see it but enjoy the attention?'

Dolores gasped, while Fern grinned mischievously.

'I'm sure I don't know what you're getting at.' Elsie got up, smoothed her gown with her hands. 'What I do know is that I don't have to listen to any more of your nonsense. Good night.' Before leaving the room she glanced over at Captain Maitland who immediately looked up. Seeing she was upset, his expression turned from one of pleasure to one of concern.

The three women exchanged a knowing look but said nothing, simply watched as Captain Maitland finished his conversation, downed his drink, and traced Elsie's footsteps.

Dolores looked down and studied her hands.

Fern used a spoon to fish out the last of the hot chocolate from her cup.

Nancy resumed her knitting. She tutted.

After a long pause Fern said, 'I think I'll leave it a day or two before confessing my undying love to Captain Maitland.'

Nancy sniggered and nodded. 'Yes, dear, perhaps you should. You know, I'm quite certain there's more going on between those two than there should be.'

Dolores let out another undignified snort of laughter. 'You two are such gossips!'

Out on the veranda, Durante had joined Sir Ernest. The conversation had been light. Sir Ernest puffed on the last of his cigar while Durante lit a cigarette. He stared at the glowing tip for a moment. Over his shoulder, beyond the glass doors, he knew Fleming hovered. He'd seen him alone at a table, one eye on his warm milk, the other on Sir Ernest.

'Is the private detective Henry Fleming working for you?' asked Durante.

Sir Ernest frowned. 'What an odd question. Of course not. D'you think I'm made of money?! And anyway, what need would I have for a private detective?'

Durante shrugged. 'I don't know. He follows you around. Not too close, but not too far away either.'

'Does he? I hadn't noticed.'

Durante tugged at his ear while thinking. 'On the other hand, perhaps he's investigating you.' He didn't smile.

'I certainly hope not. By all accounts he's a bloodhound in a Savile Row suit. I'm jesting of course; there would be no reason for him to be looking into me. My life is uneventful to say the least.'

Durante chuckled. 'You're right. Sometimes, I have quite the imagination. You'd have to have some deep dark secret for the likes of Henry Fleming to be investigating you. I've read about many of his exploits, although I'm sure the press exaggerate the details.'

'Without a doubt,' chuckled Sir Ernest. 'The press is well known for its outlandish headlines and bloated tales of adventurc.'

'I have the impression Fleming enjoys the publicity. His fame. The celebrity that comes with the high profile cases he takes on.'

'You sound a little jealous.'

'On the contrary. I'm a private man. I prefer my anonymity.'

'I'm not so sure he courts the limelight. I've only known the man a short while but from what little I've seen of him he keeps himself to himself. I suspect the newspaper headlines are unavoidable.'

'He can be quite direct. A most un-British trait in my experience.'

'You're not wrong there, Durante. The man knows how to speak his mind.'

Durante crushed his cigarette butt under the heel of his shoe. 'Well, good night, Sir Ernest.'

Sir Ernest raised and hand in acknowledgment. 'Sleep well.'

Durante started to walk away then stopped. He looked up at the stars and then at Sir Ernest. 'Venice is a beautiful city, of that there's no doubt. If you ever get the chance, you should come to my home city of Florence. I trust you've never been there?'

'No, never. I've heard it's quite beautiful.'

Durante sighed passionately. 'For me, no city compares. I hope one day you'll visit. Bring Lady Templeton. I will show you the sights and make you feel at home. Good night.'

Sir Ernest raised his glass. 'Good night, old boy.'

CHAPTER ELEVEN

ALL FINGERS AND THUMBS

Captain Maitland opened the elevator doors and stepped into the reception area. He leaned heavily on his walking stick, groaning inwardly as he put weight on his injured leg.

'Are you okay, Matty?' asked Elsie, who'd been waiting for him. 'You don't look yourself this morning.' She put a hand to his face. 'You're very pale.'

He moved away from her hand. 'I'm fine. My leg's sore that's all. All the walking and sightseeing is taking its toll. I might rest up today.'

'Are you sure that's all it is? You seem very down. Perhaps a good breakfast will set you straight?'

He looked at the concern in her warm brown eyes. He was about to say something but simply nodded instead.

'I'll help you,' she said. She held out her delicate elbow. 'Why don't you take my arm?'

'Thank you, but I'd rather not. I'll be fine.'

'As you wish. Teddy's been deep in conversation once again. I'm feeling completely ignored. He's promised to take me out. He said he'll buy me a gift. Are you sure you can't come with us? It would be lovely if the three of us went together. We could all have lunch. I know how you enjoyed those little snacks... what did you call them?'

'*Cicchetti*.'

'That's it. So you'll come?'

Captain Maitland stopped walking. He could hear the chatter from the breakfast room as they approached. 'You go ahead.'

'What's wrong? I've been waiting for you.'

'I know, and I'm grateful. But you should be with Teddy.'

'He's fine. He's chatting to all and sundry the way he does. I'd put money on the fact he hasn't even noticed my absence.'

'Even so.'

'Come on. Don't be so daft.'

'I'll be along shortly. I think a cigarette might be in order.'

'You've only just had one. What's really going on?'

'Nothing. You go and join Teddy. I need some fresh air.' He turned and walked towards the terrace.

'Why don't I join you while you have your smoke?'

'Please don't wait for me any longer. Go and enjoy your breakfast.'

Elsie put her hands on her hips and pouted. 'Oh, come on, Matty. Don't be like that.'

GERARDO'S VOICE could be heard from the breakfast room. 'I can't explain it either, Signorina Lombardi. I left my new wristwatch on my bedside table. Black face, brown leather strap. I only take it off when I sleep or bathe.'

'I can assure you. No member of our staff would steal from a guest. It's unthinkable! They would not risk losing their job.'

'Listen to me, signorina. Either one of your staff stole it, or you have a problem with thieves entering hotel guest rooms. I know I'm not the only one who's had something go missing.'

'Signor, please! We pride ourselves on our service and the security of our guests, and that includes their property.'

In the dining room, Doctor Ingrey dipped his toasted bread into his boiled egg. The golden yolk spilled down the side of the egg cup and he scooped it up with a finger. 'Cardiology,' he said. 'That was my speciality before the war, afterwards I became a GP.'

'The heart?' said Teddy.

'That's right. A cardiologist focuses on the heart, and circulatory system. Blood, blood vessels, heart; the whole kit and caboodle.'

Teddy shuddered. 'I'm squeamish about blood and what not. Have been since I was a lad. I don't know how you do it.' He pushed away his breakfast of ham, cheese and blood-red tomatoes.

'I find the whole thing fascinating. You know, I heard talk recently that it's believed one day doctors will be able to perform a heart transplant.'

'A what?'

'Did you hear what the doctor said, Ernest?' said Lady Templeton who sat at the next table with Sir Ernest. 'For goodness' sake, take your head out of the newspaper!'

In a low voice the doctor explained how he understood the procedure might be carried out.

The colour drained from Teddy's face. 'Heavens!'

Lady Templeton crossed herself. 'Surely that would be impossible?'

'It's highly unlikely it could ever work, but huge advances in medicine are happening all the time so you never know. My day to day is far more mundane. It sometimes feels like I spend most of my time taking temperatures and writing prescriptions.'

Nancy and Fern had managed only a light breakfast. Their plates of fruit and cereal remained largely untouched.

'You must eat something, Nancy.'

'I'm not hungry.'

'I understand that. We'll get some fresh air in a little while, but I'd rather you had something before we go out.'

'I want to go home, Fern. I want my own bed,' said Nancy querulously. 'I don't like it here any more. I don't like the heat, the food, or the people.' She looked around at all the guests in the dining room.

'Nance, I promise everything will be fine. You'll see.'

Nancy didn't appear reassured. 'How can you be sure?'

'You trust me, don't you?'

She nodded. 'Of course I trust you. You're my closest, dearest friend.'

'Understandably, you're a little upset. You had a nasty scare. But before that we were having a good time, weren't we?'

She nodded. 'I have been having a good time. Until last night I was enjoying myself.'

'Well, then, let's see how today goes. How does that sound?'

'If you say so, Fern. You always know what's best.'

'We look after each other when nobody else does. Isn't that our motto?'

Nancy smiled. 'We made that up when we were small girls. Do you remember?'

'When we were knee-high to a grasshopper! We were in the special camp we made in the woods. I remember.'

Nancy looked at her now soggy cereal. 'You know, I think maybe I could manage some bread and honey.'

Fleming sat alone at a table in the corner of the dining room. Despite the early hour it was sweltering and so with some hesitancy in such a formal setting, he breakfasted without his jacket, choosing instead the more comfortable attire of shirt, tie, and waistcoat. He smoothed Damson preserve onto fresh crusty bread. As he brought it up to his mouth, a purple blob of jam slid from the bread onto the sleeve of his pristine white shirt. 'My goodness!' He took a napkin and dipped a corner in his glass of water. He first dabbed and then wiped at the stain. 'Ah! I'm making a mess.'

'Good morning, Mr Fleming,' said Dolores, standing before him at the table.

'Dolores, my apologies, I'm all fingers and thumbs this morning. Look at this calamity. This is a new shirt and I'm not sure the stain will ever come out.' He gestured for her to take a seat. 'Are you all right? Has something happened?'

Dolores sat down. 'There's something I need to tell you.'

'Would you like tea?' asked Fleming. 'I always travel with my own preferred brand.' He gestured to the teapot on the table between them.

'No. Thank you.' She watched as Fleming topped up his cup.

'The milk isn't the same as in England, nor the water, which affects the taste but it's passable.'

'About last night.'

Gerardo entered the dining room with Captain Maitland, the two men deep in conversation.

'It would seem the hotel's thief has been busy again,' said Fleming. 'Be sure to secure any valuables. Hotels are a rich hunting ground for the light-fingered.'

'That's what I wanted to talk to you about. I'm a light sleeper and I think I might have heard the thief in the room next to mine.'

'What exactly did you hear?' asked Fleming with mild concern. He dipped the napkin in the glass again and tried scrubbing in a circular motion.

'I'm not exactly sure but it was a loud noise like a thud. At first I thought perhaps someone had fallen, but then the door opened and closed. I went to my door...'

'Did you see anyone?'

'I know it's silly, but a strange feeling came over me and at first I was too scared to look. After some hesitation, I opened my door just a crack and peered through.' She put a hand to her mouth. 'Thankfully, I saw no one. Though, I'm sure I heard the sound of running feet on the stairs.'

'Who is in the room next to yours?'

'Mr Durante. He wanted to talk to me so we had arranged to breakfast together this morning. He should have been here an hour ago.'

'And you haven't seen him?'

Dolores shook her head. 'No. I asked at reception and he hasn't checked out of the hotel.'

'They were certain?'

'Oh, yes, quite certain.' She thought for a moment. 'I do hope he's all right.'

Fleming examined his shirt sleeve and pulled a face of displeasure. He looked up at Dolores. 'I'm sure he's merely gone out to explore the city. Like myself, he's an early riser.' Fleming took out his pocket watch. He snapped open the case and noted the time. 'Why don't you return to Lady Templeton. I will make enquiries.'

'Thank you, Mr Fleming. That would put my mind at ease.'

Fleming remained seated while Dolores returned to her table. When she had settled he wiped his mouth carefully with a napkin. With calm and purposeful movements he rose and went to see the reception manageress, Signorina Lombardi.

CHAPTER TWELVE

INSPECTOR TROTTA

Signorina Lombardi beamed as Fleming approached the desk. 'Good morning, Mr Fleming. How can I help?'

Fleming greeted her politely then tilted his head questioningly. 'Would it be appropriate for me to offer my congratulations?'

The signorina looked confused.

Fleming added. 'Your face is glowing, your eyes are shining, you took the day off yesterday, not your usual day and... you're wearing the most beautiful diamond solitaire.' He pointed to her ring finger.

Eyes wide with delight, she held up her hand to show Fleming her engagement ring. 'My long-time boyfriend finally proposed. It was all very romantic and a wonderful surprise.'

'I'm very happy for you. My congratulations.'

Her face full of excitement she stared at her ring a moment longer then turned to Fleming. 'Forgive me. How can I assist?'

'I was wondering whether you had seen or heard from Signor Durante this morning? I'm sure there's nothing amiss but it would seem nobody has heard from him yet today and I wanted to make sure he was okay. Did he pass this way early this morning?'

'I've not seen yet him today.' She turned to Rossi, the porter, and spoke to him in rapid Italian. He replied, shaking his head. Fleming listened to their back and forth for a few moments, unsure what was being said.

'Signor Rossi will go to his room. He'll knock and check all is in order.'

Fleming interjected. 'I would really like to go with him and speak with Mr Durante. I know it's silly but it would ease Miss Frost's mind if I personally made sure Mr Durante is in *rude* health.'

The manageress frowned.

'It's an English expression. It means *good* health.'

Signorina Lombardi smiled. 'That will be fine, Mr Fleming.'

The porter chatted incessantly, telling Fleming that one day he hoped to rise to a more senior position. At the top of the stairs Rossi paused. He looked at the wall light and tutted. 'The lightbulb is gone?' He shook his head and carried on with the tale of how he hoped to one day run a hotel of his own.

Fleming listened and responded accordingly.

'We have reached the room of Signor Durante,' said Rossi. He knocked. Then knocked again. 'He must be out.'

'Would you please check the room?'

The porter gave him an uncertain look, then shrugged. He pulled out a replacement key he'd been issued and reached for the door.

Fleming's hand shot out and grabbed the young man's arm. 'One moment, if you please.' He placed a hand on the door handle and, with a gentle turn, the door opened.

'It's unlocked?' said Rossi.

Fleming eased open the door and entered the suite.

Rossi remained on the threshold, shifting uneasily from one foot to another as if he instinctively sensed something awry.

The balcony doors were open. Voile curtains moved lightly in the breeze off the canal below.

Fleming looked around the sitting room. Like a hawk his eyes took in everything. He too had a sense of unease, although he hoped the feeling was misplaced.

He moved through the room, put a hand to the bedroom door and pushed it open. The room was in darkness. In the gloom Fleming could make out

Durante, lying perfectly still. Fleming softly spoke his name as he approached. 'Signor Durante, it's Henry Fleming. I'm sorry to disturb you.'

With no response, Fleming went to the curtains and opened them.

Light filtered into the room through the slats of the shutters.

Fleming approached the bed once more but it was quite clear Durante was dead.

He lay on his back with a revolver in his hand.

Rossi let out a low pitiful moan. '*Mio Dio!* He's killed himself?' He now stood in the bedroom doorway behind Fleming, his eyes irresistibly drawn to the dreadful scene in front of him.

'It would appear so,' said Fleming. He examined the entry wound beneath Durante's chin then the gun in his hand. 'You had better notify Signorina Lombardi. She will want to contact the police.' Fleming examined the bedside table. His eyes then fell on the deepest drawer of the writing bureau which was open and empty. 'One moment, if you please.'

Rossi didn't move.

On the bedside table was a tin, a small dish on which lay two tablets, and a glass of water.

Fleming took out his silk handkerchief and examined the tin which contained more of the same tablets.

He recalled Durante mentioning his prescription for a heart condition.

Fleming muttered to himself. 'It would appear he had planned to take his medication this morning.' He leaned close to the body and examined the wound. There were a few small gold fibres attached to the stubble on his chin. His eyes fell on the armchair in the corner of the room.

'What are you looking for?' asked the porter.

'Tell me what's missing from that armchair.'

Feeling the side effects of the shock, Rossi took a moment to gather his thoughts. 'There should be a cushion.'

'Precisely.'

Fleming looked around the room but to no avail. There was no sign of the cushion.

The blue shutters which led out onto a balcony were pushed to but not quite aligned. Fleming gently pulled them open. The latch which secured the shutters when closed was missing. Fleming knelt down and discovered flecks of blue paint on the carpet. He stepped over them and out onto the balcony. Below were the waters of the canal. He examined the area carefully before returning to the room.

At the writing bureau he examined the pen and paper and finally the letter opener. The blade was scratched. Using his handkerchief he picked it up and holding it to the light he could see evidence of blue paint.

He turned to Rossi whose eyes were still fixed on the dead body. Fleming placed himself between the young porter and Durante, put his hands on his shoulders and looked him in the eyes. 'Rossi, I need your help. Do you think you can do something for me?'

'Yes, signor.' His eyes suddenly focused on Fleming.

'It's imperative the police are contacted immediately. You must speak to nobody except Signorina Lombardi who is to report a murder.'

'Murder?!' Rossi's eyes widened incredulously.

'I assure you,' said Fleming. 'Durante did not kill himself.'

When Rossi had left the room Fleming continued his careful search. He remembered something Durante had told him. He'd said he worked in construction. Yet, the Italian's hands were smooth and soft. They were not the hands of a labouring man. Durante had lied.

INSPECTOR LUIGI TROTTA'S pasta sauce-stained shirt looked as though it might burst at the seams at any moment. The buttons, which appeared to be under immense pressure, held back what would undoubtedly be an avalanche of belly should they finally surrender. Unshaven for at least three days, his tie stuffed in his trouser pocket, and one shoelace about to come undone, the inspector meandered here and there as he chewed on a pastry and slurped from a small cup of strong coffee. He peered inside the bedroom while his officers went about their examination. A young *agente*, seemingly used to the inspector's apparent apathy, held up two documents. Durante's passport, and one other he'd found in the dead man's jacket which hung in the wardrobe.

A fleeting look of surprise passed over the inspector's face but he made no comment, just continued his aimless wanderings. The pastry finished, he sucked noisily on his fingers to remove the sugary residue left behind.

Apparently tired of pacing, he made himself comfortable in an armchair. He put down his empty coffee cup and flicked through the previous day's newspaper. From time to time an officer would disturb him and, apologetically, either show him something or ask a question.

Having found nothing of interest in the newspaper, the inspector left the room and went downstairs to the hotel reception area. He took a few biscuits from a plate that had been left out on the reception desk and beckoned Signorina Lombardi to join him at a table in the bar.

'Who discovered the body?' asked Trotta.

Fleming stepped forward. 'I discovered the body. I assume you would like to interview me now?'

'Your name?'

'Henry Fleming.'

'British?' Inspector Trotta sat back in his chair and appraised Fleming while scratching his nostril with a thumb. He sniffed loudly, then popped a biscuit into his mouth. Speaking with his mouth full he said, 'You're here for sightseeing?'

'Yes,' said Fleming. He then added, 'I also happen to be a private detective.'

'I see.' Trotta brushed biscuit crumbs from his shirt and, in so doing, discovered a sauce stain which he picked at with a dirty fingernail. Without looking at Fleming he said, 'An *agente* will take a statement in a short while. There is no rush.' Unable to shift the stain he turned his attention to Signorina Lombardi who sat opposite him. His manner softened and he began chatting fondly to her.

When Fleming didn't move the inspector stopped speaking and looked up at him. 'Did you not understand my English?'

'Your English is good. I simply don't understand why, when a man has been murdered in his hotel suite, you would not contain the scene, take the names of every guest and staff member, and interview them as a matter of urgency?'

The inspector smiled apologetically at Signorina Lombardi then turned back to Fleming. 'I know who you are, Mr Henry Fleming. I don't care for you attempting to encroach on my case. I consider it... rude. I would not come to your country and begin throwing around wild, outrageous theories. Despite what you might think to the contrary, it's clear to me the death was suicide. Nothing more.'

'The missing cushion?'

'Most likely removed by housekeeping to be cleaned.'

'The fact he prepared his morning medication before committing suicide?'

'Who knows what was going through the poor man's mind last evening.'

'The visitor he had in the night?'

'He may have paid for the services of a woman. These things are not unusual, yes? All minor details my excellent officers will find answers for.'

To hide his fury, Fleming placed a hand on the pocket holding his beloved watch. 'My apologies, Inspector Trotta. My intention was not to offend merely to...'

'Then, for the time being, we're done here, Mr

Fleming. The late Inspector Antonio Durante does not need his good name besmirched by the scandal that would surely arise from any suggestion that he was murdered.'

Fleming frowned, took a step closer to Inspector Trotta. 'Durante was a police inspector?'

Trotta folded his arms on top of his bulging stomach and grinned smugly. 'So, you didn't know? He retired about a year ago. From what I heard he was an excellent inspector. It would seem the celebrated, know-everything private detective Henry Fleming was in the dark about this. What a surprise, eh?'

'Thank you, Inspector. I'll leave you to your investigation. Should you need me I'll be available to you at any time, day or night.' He gave a polite nod of the head and walked briskly away.

Moments later Fleming was sitting with Dr Ingrey. News had spread among the guests that Durante was dead and that he was in fact a retired police inspector from Florence.

'Why would Durante keep his identity secret?' asked Dr Ingrey.

'Why indeed?' said Fleming. 'I see two possibilities. Firstly, he was a private man who wished to keep his old profession out of conversation. After all, he claimed to be holidaying and there are many who behave differently around officers of the law. Secondly, though retired, he was working a case.'

'You mean investigating someone?'

'It's a possibility.'

'Who?'

'That's something I'll need to establish. However, it would seem I'm unlikely to receive assistance from Inspector Trotta. I sensed more than a little animosity, I'm afraid.'

'This is all very exciting,' said Dr Ingrey. 'I wonder if you might need an assistant? I really could do with some mental stimulation. The sights of Venice are a wonder but nothing beats a good puzzle to fire up the frontal lobe!'

'My good doctor, two fine minds are certainly better than one. Your assistance would be most welcome.'

'Where should we begin?' asked Dr Ingrey with relish.

'It's vital we proceed discreetly so as not to displease Inspector Trotta. I suspect he considers this Venetian affair already a closed case.'

PART II

MURDER CANNOT BE HID LONG

CHAPTER THIRTEEN

NO FOUL PLAY

The hotel's guests and staff had been summoned to the dining room. Inspector Trotta put his cigarette to his lips, which freed that hand to half-heartedly jab his shirt tail into his trousers. 'Is that everyone?' he asked while hoicking up the belt which hung just beneath his bulging belly.

'Yes, sir,' said a young constable who stood stiff and straight beside the door. His fresh face and immaculate uniform served only to make the inspector appear even more slovenly.

Trotta stubbed out his cigarette in a nearby ashtray and eyed a plate of pastries, but resisted taking one. 'I'll make this brief. I see no point in keeping any of us here longer than is necessary.' He smiled around at the gathering, clearly hoping his words would endear him to everyone. However, when his pronouncement was greeted with silence, after clearing his throat, he continued. 'I'm sure by now you've heard there has been a death at the hotel. Despite any rumours to the contrary it's my considered opinion there was no foul play.' His eyes locked with Fleming's for a brief moment. 'The sad truth is the retired inspector took his own life. He was discovered with the instrument of his demise in his hand. His own service revolver, which he was permitted to keep.' He stopped pacing and turned to the guests. 'Are there any questions?'

No one spoke.

Fleming could feel Dr Ingrey's eyes on him but Fleming refrained from asking any of his many questions.

'In that case,' said Trotta, picking up a pastry. 'I will leave you to enjoy the remainder of your time in our wonderful city. The beautiful Signorina Lombardi has my details. If anyone should need to contact me then please speak to her.' He grabbed a second pastry and gestured to the young constable to open the door.

When the inspector had finally left the room, leaving a trail of flaky crumbs behind him, several guests gave loud, relieved sighs.

'That was short and to the point,' said Captain Maitland. 'Not much of an orator, is he?'

'How sad though,' said Elsie. 'I only ever spoke to

Signor Durante a few times but he seemed such a lovely man.'

'I couldn't agree more,' said Teddy. 'Do you think the bar's open, Matty? I know it's early in the day but I could do with a drink after that.'

Captain Maitland leaned on his stick as he rose to his feet. 'Let's investigate.'

Nancy dabbed the tears in her eyes with an embroidered handkerchief. 'Poor man,' she murmured. 'So charming.'

Fern put an arm around her companion. 'It's so very sad. He was a lovely gentleman. We had no inkling of his troubles, did we, Nance?'

'No, dear. No inkling at all.'

Gerardo turned to Dolores, Lady Templeton and Sir Ernest. 'To me it seems so shocking that someone such as Durante would do such a thing. He simply wasn't the type.'

'I know exactly what you mean. On the surface he appeared to have a good head on his shoulders. However, there's no reason to doubt Inspector Trotta's conclusion. Despite appearances to the contrary, he seems a capable enough man,' suggested Sir Ernest. 'You know the police often keep information back from the public. It's possible Durante was down on his luck. I've a feeling there must be more to the story than

Trotta's letting on. All the same, it's a sad state of affairs. Wouldn't you say?'

Gerardo shrugged. 'I think that perhaps we should raise a glass to Durante this evening at dinner.'

'That's a lovely idea,' said Lady Templeton.

'Jolly good thinking,' agreed Sir Ernest.

Dolores had been withdrawn but she suddenly said: 'I wonder what Signor Durante wanted to talk to me about at breakfast?'

'I guess we'll never know,' said Gerardo.

'Did he give you any indication at all about what he intended to discuss? It might be of interest to Inspector Trotta,' said Sir Ernest.

She shook her head. 'He simply invited me to join him. We've talked at length about this and that. He liked to practise his English and I enjoyed listening to his stories of Florence. It sounds like a delightful city.'

Fleming did a head count. He wanted everyone in the room at the same time. He waited for Teddy and Captain Maitland, who soon returned from the bar having managed to get coffee laced with a good measure of whisky. Teddy handed one to Elsie.

From reception appeared Signorina Lombardi. She was carrying an envelope which she passed to Sir Ernest who, without much thought, opened it.

Fleming watched as the colour drained from Sir

Ernest's face and knew immediately what the envelope contained.

Lady Templeton looked over at her husband and she too instinctively realised there was a problem. She snatched it from his hand. 'It's the same as the other one.'

All guests fell silent.

Dolores placed a comforting hand on Lady Templeton's arm.

'If you'd be so kind.' Fleming held out his hand to Lady Templeton.

'You can have it; I can't bear to read any more.' She thrust the letter into Fleming's hand. Looking around she saw all eyes were on her. 'It seems the cat's out of the bag now. The whole hotel will know our secret and the threat that hangs over us.'

'I can only assume this is an unhappy coincidence,' said Fleming with a sigh. 'First Durante is discovered dead under suspicious circumstances and within a few short hours a second letter arrives.'

'I still have no idea how this person knows our whereabouts,' mused Sir Ernest.

Fleming concentrated as he examined the note with a single word: GUILTY. 'It is similar, a single word, its intention to intimidate and induce fear.' With the note was a fragment of a photograph, just a small corner with a burned edge. It was impossible to tell who was in the photograph as only the edge of a woman's dress was visible, nothing more.

'Do you recognise this?' asked Fleming, holding it up to Sir Ernest and Lady Templeton.

They both shook their heads.

'As you well know, Fleming, I pay such things scant regard, but if I ever discover who's behind this, I promise you his backside will meet the sharp end of my boot right before he's handed over to the police,' said Sir Ernest hotly.

Teddy's hand was up in the air like a school child trying to attract his teacher's attention. 'You just said that Durante was "found dead under suspicious circumstances", so I'm not quite sure what you're suggesting. Didn't Inspector Trotta just tell us it was... well, he did *himself* in?'

'Mr Fleming believes he was murdered,' said Dr Ingrey eagerly. 'A few details don't quite add up and so we're examining the case ourselves.'

'Good heavens!' said Fern. 'Is that wise?'

'I don't like the sound of that,' squeaked Nancy.

'You and Mr Fleming?' asked Gerardo.

'That's right. It's all very interesting and the way Mr Fleming explained it to me it all sounds quite plausible. It's clear the decision to rule the death suicide is entirely premature.'

Fleming examined the envelope, folded the letter

back inside and slipped them into his jacket. 'Thank you, Dr Ingrey.'

Dr Ingrey looked sheepish. 'I've perhaps blundered. My apologies, Fleming. I've jumped the gun. It wasn't my place to say anything.'

'You're proposing Durante was murdered?' asked Captain Maitland. 'Such a wild theory would seem unfounded.'

'The Italian police have closed the case,' added Dolores.

'I'm not sure it's any of our business,' said Fern.

'No, no, no! Absolutely not.' Nancy was firm. 'The police have done their job. That's the end of the matter.'

'For Durante's sake if Fleming has suspicions then surely it's his duty to investigate,' Gerardo chimed in.

'We're guests in another country. It doesn't sit right with me at all,' said Sir Ernest.

Fleming stood a little straighter and raised a hand.

The room fell silent.

'The situation is that I *will* be investigating Durante's death. I have no doubt in my mind that he was murdered. You will be interviewed by me. I understand that you may refuse my request but I would urge you most strongly to consider your position and see my inquiries as an opportunity to exonerate yourself.'

'You think one of us killed Durante?' asked

Dolores incredulously as though the idea was preposterous.

'It's a distinct possibility that at least one guest played a part in his death. I'm certain it's unlikely an outsider moved through the hotel unseen, entered the room where Durante was sleeping, murdered him, then left undetected. The more likely scenario is that a guest ended his life.'

'Some wedding anniversary this is turning out to be,' grumbled Sir Ernest.

'Does this mean we won't be able to go on any excursions?' asked Nancy anxiously.

'We were hoping to visit St Mark's Basilica again, and view the Wine Fountain Nancy's read about,' added Fern.

'For the most part your holiday activities will remain unaffected. As much as possible, I'll conduct any inquiries so as not to intrude.'

'It all sounds rather exciting if you ask me,' said Elsie. 'Though I wonder whether we're in any danger? Obviously, I have Teddy and Captain Maitland to look out for me but...'

'I would suggest precautions are taken. Until I can establish why he was murdered I have no idea of the motive and whether the killer poses a threat to anyone else. Please lock your windows and doors at night, and stay in pairs whenever possible.'

'What if I wish to leave Venice before the end of my planned stay?' asked Teddy truculently. 'Are you going to stop me?'

'I have no authority to stop you,' admitted Fleming. 'However, your absence won't prevent my investigation. It might slow it down but in the end the truth will out. Your willing cooperation would therefore be appreciated.'

Teddy felt everyone's eyes on him, including Elsie's. 'I-I-I wasn't planning on going anywhere,' he stammered. 'I was simply curious, nothing more.'

'I for one am keen to learn what really happened. After all, he was a fellow countryman,' said Gerardo. 'I thank you.'

Fleming's hand instinctively moved to the pocket watch in his waistcoat, his thumb smoothing around its familiar shape. 'I have work to do. I will discuss my concerns with Trotta's superiors and advise them of my plans to conduct a private inquiry.'

CHAPTER FOURTEEN

TROTTA HAS NO CHOICE

Inspector Luigi Trotta forked the last of the seafood pasta into his mouth. While he chewed he tipped his bowl and mopped up the garlicky sauce with a hunk of focaccia. He half-filled his mouth with the sopping bread, took a noisy slurp of red wine and continued to chomp. Wiping the drips from his stubbled chin and neck with a napkin, which he then used to wipe sweat from his forehead, the inspector forced a loud belch and sat back. He then took a grubby matchstick from his pocket and proceeded to pick his teeth, all the while looking the private detective up and down.

Fleming's air of grandeur and stiff manner did not impress Trotta. He wanted him out of his city; he couldn't have this puffed up Englishman discovering there really was something to his outlandish theory of murder. He'd be a laughing stock back at the station.

The inspector dropped his napkin into his empty bowl.

'I will allow you to continue your investigation,' he growled. 'My superiors wanted to put you on the first boat back to England but I convinced them otherwise.' This was a lie. Despite his protests he had explicit orders to extend Fleming every courtesy and to assist in any way possible.

'That's extremely generous. Your assistance will ease progress no end. I have a few questions.'

Inspector Trotta used a fingernail to attack a stubborn piece of squid still stuck in his teeth. He poured more red wine. 'Go ahead.'

'Are you aware of any private investigations that Durante was working on since his retirement?'

He shook his head. 'I asked around but nothing came up.'

'What about unsolved cases? Would he have looked into those?'

'You already know the answer to this. You reached out to your contact at the head of the *Carabinieri*.' He shifted his considerable weight and the chair creaked in protest. 'I contacted his colleagues in Florence. There was one unsolved case that plagued him. It's possible he continued looking into it. I don't see how it's relevant to what has happened here in Venice. He was vacationing. Not working.'

'About the unsolved case – what can you tell me?'

'A young woman was murdered and the case was never solved. I will have a summary of the investigation typed up and brought to the hotel before the end of the day.'

'An autopsy report for Durante and a list of medications and belongings would also be useful.'

'Anything else?' grunted Trotta.

'That will suffice for now, thank you.'

Trotta slurped his wine. 'You know, I don't like the way you went over my head. It was rude.'

'I'm sorry for that. Truly I am. I had hoped it could be avoided.'

'I get the impression you think highly of yourself Mr hoity-toity Fleming... All the same, I hear nothing but good things about you. When someone seems too good to be true, they usually are. That makes me suspicious.'

'I hope I can change your opinion of me,' said Fleming. 'A friend is a most valuable gift.'

'I expect to be kept involved at every stage,' said Trotta flatly. 'If there is an arrest... I shall be the one to make it.'

'I look forward to our next meeting. Whenever

that may be.' Fleming finished his glass of fresh apple juice. 'I'll be in touch.' He extended a hand.

Reluctantly Trotta shook it, then watched as the Englishman brushed the crown of his hat, before placing it on his head and marching off down the busy street.

Trotta was in no mood to get back to his desk. He ordered a lemon *gelato* which he guzzled while watching the passers-by.

'What do you make of all this talk of murder?' asked Dolores. She and Gerardo had joined Nancy and Fern on another visit to St Mark's Square and the Wine Fountain. The two women were a short distance away and were no doubt discussing the same topic.

'I must agree with Fleming. I too believe he was murdered,' said Gerardo. His face fell before he rallied a smile. 'Why talk about such things? We're in one of the most beautiful cities in the world, and you wish to talk about poor Durante?'

'What *would* you like to talk about then? And please don't waste your breath on more romantic nonsense. No mention of kissing beneath the stars, or dinner on a moonlit terrace. I've told you, I have no interest in men, or their boyish pursuits. And anyway, my life is full enough right now.' She gave him a stern look. It didn't matter how many times she tried to put him off, Gerardo still persisted.

He put a hand to his heart as though mortally wounded. 'You have my word. I will settle for friendship if that is all I can have.'

Dolores felt lighter and more willing to chat. 'Tell me about you. Your family. What it was like growing up as a child in Italy. What are your parents like? Do you have any siblings?'

'My life is mundane. I'd bore you and you'd never want to spend another minute with me. I have an idea. Why don't you tell me about life as a companion to Lady Templeton. Does she bathe in champagne? Is Sir Ernest really as mean as he looks?'

Dolores giggled and playfully slapped him. 'Don't say that. Lady Templeton can barely afford champagne, let alone bathe in it. They might look rich but most of the time they can barely rub two coins together. And Sir Ernest isn't mean at all. He's a teddy bear. He might growl and complain and get grumpy from time to time but isn't that what all old men do? Lady Templeton keeps in him check when he gets too self-important. You'd like Sir Ernest if you got to know him. You should have a proper conversation with him.'

'What does that mean?'

'I've noticed you avoid him. He's not all that

intimidating, you know. I find him extremely interesting to talk to. In fact, both he and Lady Templeton are very well informed when it comes to world affairs.'

Gerardo's face flushed.

'I didn't mean to embarrass you,' said Dolores.

'I'm not embarrassed,' insisted Gerardo. 'I've spoken to him, and Lady Templeton, on many occasions.'

Sensing Gerardo was upset, Dolores changed the subject. Pointing out features of the fountain she liked she talked about her time with Lady Templeton. 'She's such a lovely person. We have many similar interests. Of course, things aren't always easy. Every friendship has its ups and downs. Recently, there has been considerable tension in the air.'

'Why's that?' asked Gerardo.

'I'm not sure I should be saying.' She looked around to make sure nobody was in earshot. 'The letter they received the other day? It wasn't the first one and, from what I can gather, they're quite threatening. It would seem somebody intends to harm Sir Ernest. It's why Henry Fleming is here. I overheard a conversation and it's clear he's looking out for his well-being. It's at Lady Templeton's request.'

'That's terrible.'

'Oh, yes! The first one was waiting for him when

we arrived at the hotel. It's caused considerable distress.'

'Who would do such a thing?'

'Sir Ernest calls the person a coward.'

'He's right. We Italians prefer our disagreements to be heard. Look a man in the eye and tell him how you feel. That way you know where you stand.'

'I quite agree. This drip of hateful letters is exhausting. I feel so sorry for them both.'

'Do you know what he did to cause this person to be so upset?'

'That's the odd thing. There's never been any mention of the reason they despise him. Lord Ernest is as bewildered by the whole thing as everyone else. He wonders whether it's possibly a case of mistaken identity.'

Gerardo looked thoughtful. 'Perhaps he has a secret that not even Lady Templeton knows.'

Dolores shrugged. 'I've wondered the same thing. I can't imagine that he'd have done anything so bad that somebody feels it's all right to send such letters. After all, it's not just him that's affected. It's those around him too.'

'I can see it upsets you.' He clasped her hand between his. 'Let's talk about something else.'

'I've a better idea. Why don't we catch up with Fern and Nancy and see if they'd like to get a bite to eat. I'm famished.' She opened her purse to check she had her money with her. 'That's odd. I could have sworn I put my powder compact in my handbag.' She searched again.

'Is it valuable?' Gerardo's eyes fell on an envelope in the bag which Dolores hastily hid from view.

'It was a gift from my mother. It had been given to her by my father. It's French made and quite beautiful in design. It has a fine guilloché pattern on the outer case and at its centre is the most exquisite enamelled pink rose with green leaves.'

'I'm sure it'll turn up. You must have left it in your room back at the hotel.'

'You're right. There's no point fretting. It's not likely someone would have gone into my purse and stolen it. Who would do such a thing?'

Dr Ingrey examined the typed summary of the police report. It had just arrived, hand delivered by a fresh-faced constable. Despite Fleming's misgivings, Inspector Trotta had lived up to his word and been more cooperative than he had thought. The report was surprisingly thorough and informative. Fleming had read it twice through already.

'You're quite right, Fleming,' said Dr Ingrey. 'The

medication Signor Durante took was for a heart condition. It's very similar to something I myself would prescribe. It's usually taken at the same time each day.'

'Durante told me he took his medication every morning. I know I've said it before but I struggle to believe he placed a glass of water beside his bed and put his medication out for the morning then proceeded to end his life with his revolver. Also, using a cushion to muffle the sound so as not to disturb the other guests. A cushion, I might add, which has subsequently vanished. It's a preposterous notion!'

'When you put it like that I have to agree.'

'I will waste no more time considering his death was suicide. Any doubts I might have had have evaporated completely. I'm now convinced his death can only have been the result of a murderous act staged to look like suicide.' Fleming was saying the words out loud for his own benefit as much as for Dr Ingrey's. 'The report from Inspector Trotta serves only to underline my earlier assertions.'

'What next?' asked the doctor.

'We determine who among the guests had motive enough to want Durante dead.'

'I've chatted to all the guests and I hardly think any one of them capable of murder. To my mind it seems out of the question.'

Fleming gave a curious smile. 'We shall see whether you're right.'

'Would I be correct in thinking you have suspicions already?' The doctor adjusted his shirt collar; he could see the answer on Fleming's face. 'I suppose what I'm really asking is whether you've already ruled me out as a suspect?'

Fleming thought about his answer for a moment. 'It's been claimed in newspapers around the world that Henry Fleming is one of Britain's greatest living detectives. I'll admit I find such proclamations uncomfortable. Having read several of these articles, it's true to say that most of what is written is fanciful. In amongst the outlandish claims of my heroic exploits, there are a few interesting observations, one of which is that I have an excellent track record in solving the unsolvable...'

Dr Ingrey regarded Fleming fondly. He enjoyed his company and, having previously only observed a man who for the most part was serious and clearly relished feeling in control, he found it interesting to glimpse the great detective's discomfort at dealing with his celebrity. It made him a little bit more human. Even, perhaps, a little vulnerable.

Fleming continued. '...however, let me ask you. Would it be wise for such a great detective to rule out at this early stage a man such as yourself? A person with an intimate knowledge of the human body, and medicine. After all, we know Durante relied on pills for his heart.'

'I see,' said the doctor. 'I have to admit that makes me a little uneasy.'

'And so it should. I learned to my cost many years ago never to take anyone at face value. However, my good doctor, if it eases your mind, for the time being I feel you are an unlikely candidate for this murder.'

Dr Ingrey appeared relieved. 'Though not entirely satisfactory, it's something, I suppose. Out of interest, what makes you say that?'

'Your shoes.'

'My shoes?'

'Is it not true that you only brought with you one pair?'

The doctor looked more than a little surprised. 'Well, yes. My favourite pair.'

'Let me explain. You packed only one pair of shoes. Your most comfortable walking shoes. They are hand-made, of high quality and well worn. The leather is broken in and they no doubt fit like a glove. You look after them well and they have probably been re-soled on numerous occasions. Since arriving, I've noted you place them outside your door each evening to be cleaned and maintained by the hotel's butler. A service which I also use.'

'What on earth have my shoes to do with whether or not I'm a suspect in this case?'

'I made it a priority to speak with the butler who cleans the shoes. After all, like yourself, I place great value in owning and maintaining good shoes. Having got to know the butler, an elderly gentleman named Arturo, whose intimate knowledge of shoe care is extraordinary, he freely shared several invaluable tips from his decades of accumulated knowledge.'

By this point the doctor looked baffled. He frowned with concentration. 'I don't quite follow.'

'At the time of the murder Dolores claims to have heard footsteps on the stairs. A sound that would not have been made by bare feet and when your shoes would have been in the care of Arturo. So you see, at this moment in time, I consider it unlikely that you entered Durante's room and murdered him. The killer was not barefoot as you would have been.'

'I could well have borrowed some shoes. Or purchased some fine Italian footwear without your knowledge.'

'This is true. It's why you are not ruled out completely, Doctor,' said Fleming with a mischievous twinkle in his eyes.

Doctor Ingrey shifted uncomfortably. 'I'm glad to hear it.'

'Now we have that out of the way. We must begin

our interviews with the others. I have a feeling it will be an interesting few days ahead.'

'I quite agree.' The doctor produced a new notepad. 'I've purchased this specifically for our undertaking. I'm taking the responsibility of my duty very seriously. In fact, I plan on documenting my observations in a journal.'

'I'll be interested to read it. I'm sure it will be most beneficial.'

CHAPTER FIFTEEN

MAITLAND'S HEART

Captain Maitland eased himself into an armchair and stretched out his bad leg. He leaned his walking stick against the arm of his chair. 'I curse the day I decided to come to Venice. I look back now and wonder what I was thinking. At least in England I can achieve some level of comfort in a more temperate climate. Here, I'm not only contending with the pain but the blasted heat as well. One can't get a decent cup of tea for love nor money, and as for the food! Well, right now I'd crawl the length of this land for a humble plate of pie and mash.' He pinched the bridge of his nose. 'I'm sorry, gentlemen, I'm feeling incredibly irritable today. I really just want to be back in my Bayswater apartment.'

'I quite understand,' said Fleming. 'I too miss England and its familiarity. The sight of green rolling hills, the sound of the milkman's whistle and the post-man's bicycle bell, the smell of freshly cut grass, the taste of my housekeeper's rich fruit cake. All are a comfort to me.'

'If you'd like me to examine your leg for you, I'd be happy to do so,' said Dr Ingrey.

'Thank you, Doctor, but I'll be all right in a little while. I just took a painkiller, the discomfort will soon subside.' He reached into his pocket and took out his cigarette case. He snapped it open and offered it to the two men. Both declined. 'I had to buy a new cigarette case. Believe it or not I lost my last one. I must have put it down without thinking. A shame really. Funny how you grow attached to the little things. I liked how the old one felt familiar in my hand. Odd how you don't notice how much these familiar objects mean until they're gone.'

'Odd indeed,' said Fleming sympathetically. He left an appropriate pause before continuing. 'You don't strike me as a man who would travel all this way without first having given the idea considerable thought.'

'I'm not sure I catch your meaning, Fleming.'

'You will have known you'd be in a lot of discom-fort, and yet here you are. What's the real reason you travelled to Venice?'

Captain Maitland examined the red glowing tip of

his cigarette before answering. 'Teddy and I go back a long way. He insisted I join Elsie and himself on their little adventure. He likes having me around.'

'Yes, yes, yes. You told me this and I accepted it. However, you and I both know that unless you wanted to be here, there are a million and one excuses you could have made.'

'I knew a change of scenery would do me good. I decided the reasons for going on the trip outweighed the reasons not to.'

'There is more to it than that.'

'I was at a loose end. I needed to get away.'

'Does that need to get away have anything to do with your troubled love life?'

'Perhaps to a degree it does. But not how you might think.'

'Captain Maitland, you've hinted at your reason already. You came to me seeking counsel. You're in love with a married woman. Why not confess to me in confidence who this woman is? After all, I think anyone with half an ounce of sense has established your broken heart.'

Captain Maitland looked at Dr Ingrey with hesitancy.

'Anything said between us will be treated the same way I treat patient confidentiality. Nothing goes beyond these four walls. You have my word,' said Dr

Ingrey. He put down his pen and folded his arms as though he was about to listen to a patient.

'I don't see how this is relevant to your investigating Durante's death?'

'Let me be the judge of that,' said Fleming.

Maitland groaned inwardly. 'I'm in love with Elsie. There, I said it. I'm in love with Teddy's wife, and he's my best friend. Now I ask you: what type of fool and a cad does that make me?'

Fleming and Dr Ingrey looked at Captain Maitland with sympathy.

Captain Maitland angrily rubbed his aching leg. 'I'm enduring this misery to be close to her. She has no idea how I feel and, of course, it has to stay that way. I can't risk losing Teddy's friendship, or hers.'

'You have my word,' said Fleming.

'Mine too,' said Dr Ingrey.

'Now, tell me what you know of Durante. You spoke to him on several occasions. I got the impression you and he got on well.'

'He was a nice fellow. A dry sense of humour, I suppose you'd call it. We talked about this and that.'

'Did you speak about anything specifically?'

'Not really. We chatted about pretty much anything. He asked a lot of questions. In fact once I learned he was a police inspector I wasn't at all surprised.'

'Why do you say that?'

Captain Maitland thought about it for a moment. 'It was the way he asked his questions and the nature of them, I suppose. He was interested in the other guests. He'd ask what I knew about them. I explained I didn't know them before reaching Venice. Except Teddy and Elsie, of course. We talked about the war and coming home. He was very interested in England. He suggested he might like to visit. Naturally, I offered to put him up if he was ever in London.'

'Did he ever mention knowing any of the guests himself?'

'He might have done but, off the top of my head, I can't recall him doing so.'

'What do you do for a living, Captain?'

'When I return to England I plan on teaching English. I have some inheritance money and savings I've been living off but that won't last for ever and so I decided I need to get a job. My grandfather was the headmaster at a village school. I thought I'd follow in his footsteps. I'll find somewhere quiet and hide away for a while.' He smiled wistfully. 'I hope I can make my grandfather proud. Maybe I'll even find myself a sweet country girl to marry. Someone who'll take my mind off Elsie.'

'I think that would be worth your serious consideration.' The men sat in silence for a moment. 'If I might return to the question of Durante's death: did you see anyone enter or leave Durante's room on the night he was murdered?'

Captain Maitland pursed his lips thoughtfully. 'I can't say that I did.'

'On the morning of the murder, if memory serves, Elsie was not at breakfast with Teddy. I assume she was with you and this was why she was late?'

Captain Maitland frowned and sounded angry. 'I came to breakfast after Elsie and Teddy. I was unaware she was late and have no idea why that would be. She was waiting for me. She fusses over me. She does it because she cares for me... as a friend. The truth is I've become too fond of her attentions. And so, that morning, I pushed her kindness away. I was rude. Ungrateful. There's nothing more to it than that. I hope you're not suggesting she and I...'

Fleming smiled soothingly. 'I meant nothing by my question. I apologise if I was indelicate. I'm simply trying to establish everybody's whereabouts.'

'I might be a little quick to bite. Listen, my concern is that the moment I admit my feelings I'm hit with accusations of impropriety. That's something I can't bear. It's something I won't have. Elsie's reputation is on the line.'

'Quite so,' said Fleming. 'Thank you for your time. I needed to be certain you weren't together. I now fully understand the delicacy of the situation. You've been most enlightening.'

The door closed behind Captain Maitland and Dr Ingrey let out a sigh of relief.

'I had no idea your work was so filled with tension. The captain is an interesting and complex character,' said Dr Ingrey, keeping his head down as he made notes on his new notepad.

'He did get a little riled,' said Fleming.

'You can say that again. I thought for a moment he might clock you right on the nose.' The doctor leaned back in his chair and put his hands behind his head.

Fleming put a hand to his nose. 'He wouldn't be the first.'

The doctor's eyes widened. 'Really?'

Fleming raised his eyebrows and chuckled. 'If I get a reaction such as that it's simply a sign I'm asking the right questions.'

'By the look on your face I'd say you think that interview went well?'

Fleming nodded. 'We now know for certain that Captain Maitland and Elsie Kelleher aren't having an affair.'

'We do?'

'He made a big song and dance about admitting his feelings for her. He expressed his remorse for having those feelings and suggested he would run away to the country and marry a country girl. I believe more than ever he's hopelessly in love with Elsie Kelleher but has not confided in her. The truth lay in his angry reaction when I insinuated he was alone with Elsie the morning of the murder. He's protecting her. At no point did he suggest *she's* in love with *him*. In fact he denied they were together. I've observed his behaviour over time and I see the way he looks at her and the way she looks at him. It's very different. It's clear to me she sees him as a friend. Nothing more. I witnessed Elsie's manner the morning of the murder. She walked into the dining room alone. Her eyes lit up and sparkled when she sat down with Teddy. There was a quick glance over her shoulder before joining her husband. No doubt looking for Captain Maitland. However, her look was one of concern. The way someone might look out for a friend, or brother. Nothing more. I've witnessed many lovers concealing their illicit affairs, and unless I am very much mistaken the longing for more than friend-ship is one-sided.'

'Good heavens!' said Dr Ingrey. 'All this going on around me and I had no clue. I've a lot to learn.'

Fleming entered the tiny restaurant, followed closely by Dr Ingrey. The waiter showed them to a small round table in the coolest corner of the room, brought them drinks, bread, cheese and finely sliced prosciutto. Despite the lunchtime rush being as good as over, the restaurant was still full of customers enjoying conversation and finishing drinks.

Sitting shoulder to shoulder, like dormice in a nest, Nancy and Fern watched Fleming and Dr Ingrey as they took their seats on the opposite side of their table.

'I'm not at all sure we'll be able to help but we're more than willing to answer your questions, aren't we, Fern?'

'Yes, we are. We'll do what we can.' Fern gave Nancy's hand a squeeze.

The two women nodded, their round faces turned to Fleming, large wide eyes staring intently.

'There's nothing too formal about all this,' said Fleming. 'We'll simply chat. I'll ask a few simple questions and you do your best to answer as fully and truthfully as you can.'

The two women looked at each other. They linked arms. 'Yes. We can do that,' declared Fern.

Dr Ingrey crossed one leg over another and rested his notepad on his thigh.

'Dr Ingrey here will take some notes. Is that okay?' said Fleming.

'Yes. We don't mind Dr Ingrey being here.'

'We get along like a house on fire, don't we?' said Dr Ingrey.

'Of course we do,' said Nancy. She swallowed hard. 'I saw the person what did it,' she blurted suddenly.

Fern sighed. 'Oh dear, Nance. You're supposed to wait until Mr Fleming asks the questions. Now everything's all topsy-turvy.'

'I'm sorry, Fern. It just came out,' Nancy said apologetically, her bottom lip beginning to quiver.

'Don't get yourself all upset. Just wait for Mr Fleming to ask before you answer. Okay?'

'I understand, Fern.'

'What exactly do you mean when you say you "saw the person that did it"?' asked Fleming.

'Start at the beginning,' said Fern. 'Just like we talked about.'

'They'll think I'm silly,' muttered Nancy, toying anxiously with the strap of her handbag.

'No. They won't.'

'You don't believe me, so why would they?'

'I never said I don't believe you. I just think...'

Fleming interjected. 'Why don't you tell us your story? I promise to listen carefully.'

Nancy tightened her lips as she concentrated. 'It was because I got peckish you see. In the middle of the night my tummy rumbles and I can't sleep. I usually have a biscuit or two by the side of the bed but I'd forgotten them. I called out to Fern but she didn't have any.'

'We share a room,' explained Fern. 'I suggested she try to sleep and see if she could wait until breakfast.'

'Try as I might I couldn't get back to sleep, so I put on my clothes and went down to reception to ask for a little snack.'

'You went alone?' asked Fleming.

'Fern had gone back to sleep and I didn't want to wake her. I planned on being very quick. It's not the first time I've had the tummy-rumbles in the early hours. At home I like to have some rice pudding when I wake up at night, don't I, Fern?'

'You certainly like rice pudding,' agreed Fern. 'The

hotel staff have always been very accommodating with her food cravings.'

'Very kind indeed,' agreed Nancy. 'There was some soup that the kitchen staff said I could have, so I sat and slurped that.'

'What time was this?'

'I must have got out of bed around one a.m.,' said Nancy. 'And finished my soup just before two a.m. Then I went back upstairs to bed.'

Fern squeezed Nancy's arm.

'That's when I saw Signor Durante's killer,' said Nancy. 'Mr Fleming, it was a ghost what done it. I know because when I turned the corner at the top of the stairs I saw it whooshing towards me.'

Dr Ingrey stared at the two women. 'A ghost?'

'What did this ghost look like?' asked Fleming. He spoke as though ghosts were a regular occurrence in his line of work.

'It all happened so fast it's hard to say, and I was very sleepy, but it was big, and came at me like it meant to harm me,' said Nancy, her voice trembling as she recalled the horror of the encounter.

'It was me who found her,' said Fern. 'She'd collapsed outside our door. If I hadn't woken she might have stayed there all night.'

'Why didn't you contact me,' asked Dr Ingrey. 'You might have hurt yourself.'

'We don't like to be a bother, Doctor. She came to as soon as I gave her a little shake and I helped her back to bed. I gave her a tot of whisky to steady her nerves and she eventually drifted off to sleep.'

'All the same,' said Dr Ingrey. 'A shock like that would have been worth checking out.'

'I've since read there are lots of ghosts in Venice,' said Nancy. 'It's given me the right willies, I can tell you, Mr Fleming, and I'm too scared to walk about the hotel on my own any more.'

'Now you're talking silly,' said Fern sternly. 'I'm sure there's a simple explanation. And anyway, ghosts don't mean anyone any harm. Isn't that right, Mr Fleming?'

'I have little doubt you saw something, or someone, that night. I can say with some measure of certainty though that your encounter was *not* of a supernatural nature.'

'I told you,' said Fern. 'Your imagination's running away with you again.'

Dr Ingrey, who had been enthralled by the story, realised he'd not made any notes and suddenly began writing furiously. 'Did your ghost say anything?'

Nancy began wringing her fingers. 'Not that I can recall.'

'Can you say from which direction the figure you

saw had come and where it was headed?' asked Fleming.

Nancy closed her eyes as if recalling the scene, then shook her head. 'No, I can't be really certain of anything. It was only afterwards I realised why it went for me. It must have been hovering around the hall-ways, the way they often do. When I got to the top of the stairs it saw me! I must have startled it. That's when it rushed towards me. I was so scared my head began to spin and that's when everything went dark. The next thing I remember is Fern putting me to bed.'

'It was all so frightening for her.'

'I'm sure it was,' added Dr Ingrey. 'You're telling us you fainted?'

'That's right, Dr Ingrey. I fainted.'

'She knocked her head as well,' said Fern. 'She had a bump the size of a plum.'

'I do wish you'd come to me sooner,' said Fleming. 'However, I'm pleased you felt able to share it with me now.'

The two women looked at one another.

'We both decided it sounded rather unusual. We're aware that not everyone believes in ghosts the way we do. However we knew that you, being a broad-minded man of the world, wouldn't immediately dismiss the story, and consider us foolish. We thought you'd want to know,' said Fern.

'Also, now you know Signor Durante's death is down to a ghost it'll probably save you a lot of time,' added Nancy.

Fleming made the appropriate noises. 'I shall certainly give your encounter a lot of thought.'

'I feel ever so relieved,' said Nancy.

'Me too,' said Fern.

The waiter brought more drinks and the conversation became more relaxed. Dr Ingrey began talking about his life as a doctor. He told some stories and the two women laughed. Fleming noted the doctor's natural manner, his assuredness, and the way he put people at ease.

'That's an unusual handbag,' said Fleming to Nancy.

The bag was on her lap and as usual she had her hand on it. 'It's Nile crocodile leather.'

'It's certainly unique-looking.'

'It's hand-made,' said Nancy proudly. 'It has my initials on it. I had it made specially by a very clever man when we were in India.'

Fern gave Nancy a gentle nudge with her elbow. Nancy held it up for Fleming and the doctor to see.

'Rarely lets it out of her sight,' said Fern. 'It's very precious to her.'

Fleming put out a hand. 'May I?'

Nancy gave Fern an uncertain look.

'It has many private items inside,' said Fern. 'You know how we women are with our handbags.'

'I wouldn't dream of looking inside without your permission,' said Fleming. 'I'd simply like to hold it. I appreciate quality and it looks exceptionally well made.'

With some hesitancy Nancy passed the bag to Fleming.

'Goodness me, it's heavy!' Fleming ran a hand over the leather, closely examined the stitching and silver fastening. He squeezed it gently and ran a finger over the bumps and texture of the pattern. 'Exquisite,' he said as he handed it back.

Nancy looked relieved.

'When were you in India?' asked Dr Ingrey. 'I'd very much like to visit one day.'

Fern thought about it for a moment. 'It must have been over five years ago now. We didn't stay long. A month was enough. It's an amazing place, but quite overwhelming.'

'We left in a hurry,' added Nancy animatedly. 'In the dead of night! We caught a boat that was leaving immediately. I barely had time to pack. It was all very exciting.'

Fern looked at Nancy with annoyance. 'It wasn't as dramatic as she's making out. There was an opportunity to gain passage on a boat that was departing earlier than we first planned. It was sailing for England the same day so we took the opportunity. As you've just learned, Nancy loves a bit of the melodrama.'

Fleming watched the two women closely.

'Travelling can present many challenges. Not least of which being how costly it can be,' said Dr Ingrey.

'We do all right for ourselves,' said Nancy.

'We're not extravagant in our spending by any means,' added Fern. 'There are ways to travel on a modest income if you know what you're doing.'

'Your knowledge of such things puts me to shame, ladies,' said Dr Ingrey.

'The doctor's right. It's quite apparent to me that you're a team with quite remarkable resolve and ingenuity.'

Nancy beamed. 'That means a lot coming from you two clever gentlemen.'

Fern turned to Nancy. 'Why don't you drink up. It's time we were getting back to the hotel.'

'We can walk you back,' said Dr Ingrey. 'Isn't that right, Fleming?'

'There's no need for that, Doctor, we'll be just fine.'

Fleming sipped his drink as the two women headed off arm in arm.

'What a lovely couple,' said the doctor. 'Don't you agree?'

'They're quite the double-act, that's for sure,' said Fleming.

'Mind you, I don't know what to make of their fanciful story about a ghost having killed Durante.'

Fleming raised an eyebrow. 'There is a more logical explanation that will become apparent in due course.'

'I certainly hope so,' chuckled Dr Ingrey. 'I'm not sure what Inspector Trotta would make of you presenting him with an apparition as the main suspect in the case!'

'I'm suddenly in the mood for something sweet. I wonder if I can order a rum baba or *pasticciotto*?' Fleming's eyes fell on a plate of delicious looking sweets being delivered to another table. 'I might order that. Would you care to join me, Doctor?'

CHAPTER SEVENTEEN

UPSTAIRS, DOWNSTAIRS

D r Ingrey poured the tea. 'You know something Fleming, I have to admit, I'm in agreement with Captain Maitland. As much as I've enjoyed visiting this splendid part of the world, the culture, food, the warmth, and the sunshine, I'm rather looking forward to returning to rainy old Blighty.'

'There's a lot to be said for the familiarity of home.'

'I was telling Gerardo last night at that music bar I visit, all about my quiet little English village when all of a sudden I felt quite homesick. I think the wretched business of Durante's murder has a lot to do with it. It's foolish of me, I know.' He sipped his tea. 'We really must drag you along to listen to the music. It's quite invigorating. It might do you good to take your mind off the case for a few hours? I'm getting to know some of the regulars now and we have a good old time.'

'Gerardo was with you last night?'

'For a short while. He left early.' Dr Ingrey rubbed his jaw thoughtfully. 'Come to think of it, I also saw Durante there the evening before he died.'

'You did?'

'He was sitting in one of the quieter corners drinking alone. It was clear he wasn't himself.'

'Did anyone join him?'

Dr Ingrey thought for a while. 'For the most part he kept himself to himself. Sir Ernest showed his face. He was cheerful and bought me a drink. Then he excused himself and sat briefly with Durante. I got the feeling he wasn't much in the mood for socialising and I was right. Sir Ernest left quite soon after.'

'How did Durante appear to you after that?'

'I couldn't really say. He continued to sit alone, shunning company, and I never really paid him much attention. I was there to enjoy the evening. He'd clearly upset Sir Ernest, however.'

'Why do you say that?'

'Durante showed him something. I briefly glimpsed a necklace that he held up.'

'Sir Ernest didn't mention this to me. I wonder if he's planning a surprise gift for Lady Templeton?'

'If that's the case they didn't agree a price. The old

chap had a face like thunder. At the time it seemed to me Sir Ernest had gone out of his way to speak with Durante and it wasn't welcome. Durante could be a very serious sort. It seemed odd to me he was there at all; he didn't appear to be enjoying the music.'

'Did Durante meet with anyone else that evening?'

'A little later Captain Maitland bought a few drinks and he sat with him. They seemed to get along well. Later Teddy and Elsie appeared. Teddy was on good form. Elsie insisted he dance with her and to his credit he gave it a go.'

'And what of Captain Maitland?'

'You know I think he might have left early. Now we understand his feelings towards Elsie that would make sense. After a few drinks the poor chap must have had a hard time of watching Elsie and Teddy so in love and carefree.'

'Did Gerardo make an appearance?'

'He might have done. If I'm honest I spent most of the evening focused on the music. Considering the number of drinks consumed I'm surprised I've remembered as much as I have.' He examined his fingernails. 'On top of that, once again, for the most part I chatted to the beautiful bar owner.'

'There's no need to be coy about that, Doctor,' chuckled Fleming. 'You're only human. Romantic surroundings, uplifting music, and the company of an attractive, interesting, and unattached woman sounds like a quite perfect evening.'

'You know, Fleming, I couldn't agree more. As homesick as I might feel at times, the stories of her life both fascinate and transport me to another time and place.'

'You sound quite smitten.'

'I shall certainly be sad to say my farewells when I do eventually leave. It's made me reassess my priorities. I thought I was quite satisfied with my lot but I'm beginning to wonder whether a companion should be on the cards.'

'My friend, that's something only you can decide.' Fleming became serious. 'Something has occurred to me. You and I both use the butler service to have our shoes cleaned and our suits pressed.'

'Of course. And an excellent job Arturo makes of it, I might add,' said Dr Ingrey. 'I imagine all the guests use the service. Why do you ask?'

'It's nothing.' He waved away his partially formed thoughts. 'I've been considering flecks of blue paint. I keep wondering whether they are of importance. There is also the matter of our ghost, which we must attend to.' Fleming got to his feet. 'I must take a short walk to aid the ordering of my thoughts. I'll meet you at the top of the stairs in twenty minutes.'

Having completed a brisk stroll around a now familiar circuit of paths and alleyways, Fleming returned to the hotel and waited a few steps down from the top of the main staircase. 'Are you ready?' he called out.

'Just give me the word,' Dr Ingrey replied.

'Go!' called Fleming. With this command he proceeded up the last few steps of the hotel staircase at a leisurely pace. He reached the top of the stairs and turned. As he did so Dr Ingrey came bounding towards him. They almost collided. Fleming took a step backwards and bumped into the wall to allow the doctor to pass down the corridor to the stairs and the other rooms on the floor below.

A moment later the doctor returned. 'How was it that time?'

'Much better. Once more. This time get closer as you pass and deliberately push me aside.'

'Are you sure?'

'Quite certain.'

They returned to their positions and repeated the exercise. On this occasion the doctor deliberately brushed Fleming with his arm causing him to lose his balance and slump to the floor.

'Are you all right?' said Dr Ingrey. He put out a

hand and helped Fleming to his feet. 'I do apologise, I appear to have drastically misjudged my footing. I know you said to get close but I overdid it. Let me have a look at your head. I heard it thump on the wall behind you.'

Fleming rubbed the back of his head. 'I'm absolutely fine, Doctor, thank you. That was perfect.' He looked around and stared at the wall light behind the doctor. Then at the next one, further down the stairway. 'The bulb was missing. I recall the porter, Rossi, mentioning it.'

'Meaning Nancy, already tired, would have come from darkness into light,' said Dr Ingrey.

Fleming agreed. 'Her eyes would have had to adjust as she rounded the top of the stairs. She would have been in almost complete darkness until then and would have been startled to encounter someone so late at night coming out of the light.'

'I must agree, Fleming. She would have been shocked. It could have appeared quite ghostly.'

'Let's not forget the fact she was tired. It was the early hours of the morning. She looks up at a figure moving at speed through the light and was knocked backwards causing her head to hit the wall.'

'She could well have passed out for a moment or two.'

'I think that's very likely, Doctor. When she came

round, her mind tried to rationalise what had happened and it manifested the blur of the rushing figure and the bright light into something ghostly and sinister.'

'Her imagination played tricks on her,' said Dr Ingrey. 'I'll admit I've come to the conclusion that Nancy might be considered one of life's eccentrics.'

The two men turned at the sound of footsteps.

'I thought I heard your voice, Fleming,' boomed Lord Ernest. 'What the blazes are you up to?'

'Fleming had the idea of re-enacting the...' began Dr Ingrey.

'Would now be a convenient time for yourself and Lady Templeton to sit down with me?' interrupted Fleming.

Sir Ernest looked at Fleming and then at the doctor. Sir Ernest's shirt collar was open and his shirt sleeves rolled up. Fleming had seen him dressed this way while exercising in the courtyard.

'You have some very odd ways about you, Mr Fleming, but you appear to know what you're doing. Anyway, that's why I'm here. My wife suggested I come to get you. There's something we think you'll want to see.'

Fleming turned to Dr Ingrey. 'It would be best if I see Sir Ernest and Lady Templeton alone on this occasion.'

Dr Ingrey suddenly seemed at a loss as to what to do with himself. 'I'll write up my notes.'

'Thank you, Ingrey.' Fleming removed a small ornate tin from inside his jacket. He lifted the lid, took out some walnuts and sultanas and popped them into his mouth. He replaced the lid and handed the tin to the doctor, along with his room key. 'Would you be so kind as to put this in my room. On the bedside table would be perfect. Be sure to lock the door when you leave, then return my key to Signorina Lombardi for safekeeping. Then would you find Nancy and Fern and explain to them our findings here this afternoon. I'm sure they'll be interested to hear the results of our experiment. Apologise to them, if you'd be so kind, tell them where I am and that I might be quite some time. Should any other guests also enquire as to my where-abouts please inform them I will be available later.'

WHEN FLEMING and Lord Ernest arrived at the hotel's small reading room, Lady Templeton was sitting in an armchair reading a days' old English newspaper.

One wall of the room was dedicated to shelves with books that ranged from horticulture to horology, astronomy to zoology and a large selection of fiction.

In a locked glass cabinet, in the darkest corner, were housed rarer books and first editions.

'I thought we'd have some privacy in this quaint room, Mr Fleming. I'd rather what we're about to discuss was done away from eavesdroppers.'

Fleming took his seat opposite Lady Templeton. Sir Ernest stood close to a tall, narrow window that overlooked the canal below.

'Must you smoke, Ernest?' asked Lady Templeton sharply, her look full of disapproval. 'You're smoking far too much of late. You know how I dislike it.'

'It's one of my few vices, my dear,' insisted Ernest. 'I'll open the window.' He unfastened the latch and tried to push the window open, to no avail. 'I think it's jammed.'

Seeing his wife's face become stonier than ever he reluctantly put away his cigarettes. He pulled an armchair close, and sat between Fleming and Lady Templeton.

'Before we proceed I need to make something perfectly clear, Mr Fleming. I'm not sure that I wholeheartedly approve of your getting involved in this business with Signor Durante. I hired you to ensure my husband's safety. Yet, as far as I can see, you and the doctor are off gallivanting around investigating the death of this complete stranger, and a foreigner to boot. My husband and I are paying you good money and I expect your full attention in return.' Her eyes were full of anger. She turned to her husband. 'Do you have anything to add?'

'Well, um. I...'

'Were you even listening, Ernest?' snapped Lady Templeton. 'Take your head out of the clouds. This situation of yours isn't simply going to resolve itself, you know.'

Fleming raised a reassuring hand. 'Before I answer, I would like to first check that you have received no more of those hateful letters.'

'Not a dicky-bird,' said Sir Ernest.

'Good. And do you still have the letters that arrived during your stay here? I believe I returned them to you after my private examinations were completed.'

'Yes,' said Lady Templeton.

'Are you certain neither are missing?'

She opened her handbag and held them up for Fleming to see. 'I carry both of them with me. I'd rather a maid didn't come across them in our room. Now, can we return to the matter at hand and your obvious lack of concern for my husband's safety.'

'Please, let me explain. I was keen that Signor Durante's death should not intrude upon the work I'm undertaking on your behalf. Despite the sham of an investigation being led by Inspector Trotta, it remained none of my business. Yes, though it chills me to the bone to see something so blatantly mishandled, the truth is, I cannot involve myself in every crime I encounter.'

'Your reassurances are clearly nonsense, as you've chosen to investigate anyway.' Lady Templeton eyed him astutely. 'I inherited my mother's keen intuition, Mr Fleming. It has served me well over the years. I sense you're holding something back. What is it?'

Fleming replied with aplomb. 'It's my belief that the two cases are connected.'

Lady Templeton and Sir Ernest looked at each other with surprise.

'Are you sure?' asked Sir Ernest. 'Connected how?'

'I need more time to establish with any degree of certainty how they're connected but if you'll permit me some leniency I'll continue my investigation and confirm my suspicions in due course.'

'You must be able to give us more than that, Fleming,' said Sir Ernest. 'We're paying you good money to ensure I don't wind up dead at the hands of some letter-writing lunatic, and now you tell us a retired Italian police inspector from Florence, whom we've never met until coming here, has some connection to the death threats I'm receiving. It all sounds rather fanciful to me, I must say.'

Lady Templeton bit down on her thumbnail as she weighed up the situation. 'I don't suppose you can give us any indication of how these suspicions arose?'

Fleming tilted his head apologetically. 'That wouldn't be prudent at this moment in time.'

'Prudent? If you have suspicions then surely you should be sharing them with us. Isn't that what we're paying you for? No disrespect intended, Fleming, but if you're not going to play the game then why don't we dispense with your services altogether. It's costing me a fortune.'

'Hush now, Ernest! Stop behaving like an old goat. I don't know what's got into you. There's no point throwing the baby out with the bathwater.'

'My fee is to keep you alive, and out of harm's way, Sir Ernest. It appears to me that you remain fit as a fiddle.'

Lord Ernest puffed out his cheeks and grumbled. 'What about the letter writer, surely you can let on as to whether you're any closer to identifying them?'

'I'm very close to establishing their identity.'

'That's something I suppose.'

'Well... we'd be foolish to doubt you,' said Lady Templeton amicably. 'You're the expert when it comes to such matters.'

'There was something you wished to show me?' said Fleming.

Lady Templeton nodded encouragingly to her husband.

Sir Ernest shoved his hand into his pocket. 'I found this in our bedroom.' He released his clenched fingers. In the open palm of his hand was a gold cufflink. 'I have no idea where it's come from or what its meaning is.'

'Have you spoken to reception? It may belong to someone from housekeeping.'

'Only the maid has visited our room and it doesn't belong to her.'

'What about Dolores? Could she have dropped it?'

'She didn't recognise it. Someone other than hotel staff has been in our room,' insisted Lady Templeton.

'Was anything of value stolen?'

Sir Ernest shook his head. 'Only my diary has gone.'

'Not a single piece of jewellery is missing, Mr Fleming. Only Sir Ernest's diary. It makes no sense at all.'

'I assume it never leaves the room and remains on the writing bureau at all times?' asked Fleming.

'Quite so,' said Sir Ernest. 'Listen here, Fleming. I'll admit this has shaken me a little. This has to be the same person who's been targeting me. You're also now telling us this person might be Durante's killer.'

'Don't jump to conclusions, dear,' said Lady

Templeton. 'There could be many reasons your journal was taken.'

'Does it contain financial records, or anything... compromising?' enquired Fleming.

'Nothing of that nature. It's no more than a record of each day. Lady Templeton and I will often look through it together at the end of each year and reminisce. Who would lift something of so little value when there are jewels to be had? I tell you, Fleming, I'm getting rather angry and frustrated with it all.'

'Calm down, Ernest. Getting emotional won't help.'

Fleming placed the gold link in his pocket for safe keeping. 'I shall give this matter some thought.' He was about to leave when he noticed the cushion on the armchair; gold and turquoise with a peacock embroidered onto it.

'Is everything all right?' asked Lady Templeton.

'Yes. I have the exact same cushion in my own room. My mind is unclear as to whether a missing cushion is important or a distraction.'

Sir Ernest and Lady Templeton looked at each other with confusion.

Fleming took out his pocket watch and checked the time. 'If you'll excuse me, I have another appointment.'

CHAPTER EIGHTEEN

A NOTE OF TRUTH

Dolores twirled the parasol resting on her shoulder. Her red hair shone each time it caught the light. She and Fleming crossed the piazza. They had been walking and chatting for around an hour and after some initial caution Dolores had begun to open up.

'So you see, Mr Fleming, as much as I adore Lady Templeton, I think it's time I moved on. There's so much more I'd like to experience. What do you say?'

'It's really not my place to advise you on how to live your life, Dolores. I do understand your feeling that you've outgrown your current position as her ladyship's companion. I also acknowledge that it will be difficult. I've witnessed first-hand how close the two of you are. She values your friendship a great deal. It's why I also think that though she'll be disappointed,

I'm certain she'll understand and support your decision.'

'Do you really think so? I'd be hurt if she thought me ungrateful. She and Lord Ernest have been so very good to me.'

'I assure you. They will understand.'

Dolores gave a huge sigh of relief. 'You're so wise and easy to talk to, Mr Fleming. I feel giddy at the prospect of new adventures. I'll sit down with Lady Templeton and explain my decision at the first opportunity upon our return to England. I'll work my notice, and then return home to Portsmouth for a short while. It's so long since I've visited my parents, and my two brothers will be tickled to see me again. I might even come to visit you at Avonbrook Cottage. I'd love to meet your housekeeper Mrs Clayton and your dog, Skip. Perhaps you'd show me around the gardens you've talked so much about.'

'That would be a delight.'

'Then I'll catch a train to Wales, or Scotland, or jump on a boat to Ireland. There are so many places to explore, I'm not sure where I'll start!'

On the other side of the quaint piazza they found a shady bench upon which to sit.

'If I may, I'd like to ask you about the night Signor Durante died,' said Fleming.

Dolores closed her parasol and turned to Fleming.

'What do you need to know?'

'You said you heard noises coming from his room. I'd like you to think back and try to remember whether you heard voices. Did you hear Durante talking to anyone?'

Dolores closed her eyes and concentrated. 'I was jolted awake by a noise. A thump. As I lay in my bed I listened for what had woken me. I'm almost certain I didn't hear anyone talking. I heard footsteps moving around his room, drawers closing, and Durante's room door open and close and that's when I jumped out of bed and with some trepidation, my heart pounding, I opened my door to look out. I heard footsteps but saw nobody. That's it.'

'You're sure?'

'Certain. I'm sorry I can't help more. If only I hadn't been such a coward and looked sooner I might have seen the person responsible.'

'You've done very well.'

'There is one small thing.'

'Yes?'

'As I was closing the door, I thought I might have heard a second person. It was either more footsteps or an echo. The hotel was of course very quiet at that time but I'm fairly certain I heard more than one person on the stairs.'

'That helps me more than you realise.'

'Oh? That *is* good to know. I've been feeling quite useless. I so wish I'd seen the face of the person coming out of the room. If only I hadn't hesitated.'

'You mustn't think that way. Your instincts were correct. You didn't put yourself in harm's way. Had you jumped out of bed and thrown caution to the wind the outcome might have been very different for you. I'm pleased to say you're here to assist me today because you were careful.'

'My mother always says "The careful foot can walk anywhere". I've always thought it was a silly little saying. But now I understand what she means.'

'Your mother is a wise woman who naturally worries for the safety of her children.'

'With a head-strong daughter, and two stout-hearted sons, she has every right to fret,' chuckled Dolores. She sighed happily. 'I must say it's been most enjoyable exploring the piazza and chatting as friends.'

They sat for a while before walking back to the hotel.

'Do you have any inkling as to who's sending the items to Sir Ernest?'

'My focus at the moment is on the *why*. I believe I understand the connection between the items, and perhaps the reasoning behind it. I must now establish who the sender is.'

'Good heavens! You have been busy.'

'I have several theories, none of them pleasing. What concerns me most is how each ties in with Durante's death.'

'Oh, dear,' said Dolores. 'You seem quite distressed.'

Fleming took her hand. 'Please don't worry yourself. I succumb to these little moments of concern from time to time. I have no doubt I will shortly be able to conclude this business. Lady Templeton showed me the gold cufflink you found in their room.'

'It's very strange, and quite worrying, to think an uninvited visitor was in their room.'

'When you found the cufflink, did you find anything else?'

Dolores stopped walking. Wide-eyed she turned and looked at Fleming. She brushed a stray curl of red hair away from her forehead. 'How did you know?'

'It was merely a guess.'

'I don't believe that for one minute.' She hesitated. 'We were all returning to the room. Lady Templeton and I were planning on writing some letters home together while Sir Ernest intended changing his clothes and going back downstairs to the bar for some drinks. I'd gone ahead to draw a bath for Lady Templeton. I was in their room alone to begin with. They were close behind. I entered the room and there was an envelope on their bed. The same sort they'd received before.

They'd been in fine spirits all evening and I knew it would upset them, so I hastily grabbed the envelope, opened their window, and was about to toss it out when I thought better of it. Instead, I tucked it inside my blouse.'

While she spoke she opened her purse, where she now kept it for safekeeping, and handed it to Fleming.

'I closed the window and acted as if nothing was amiss. It was then, as they entered the room, that I noticed the glint of the cufflink. I picked it up and handed it to Lady Templeton.'

'Neither she nor Sir Ernest recognised it as a piece of their jewellery.'

'That's correct. I presumed it had been dropped by the maid. It turned out, once they'd checked, that it hadn't. I then felt unable to tell them about the new letter. I felt guilty about what I'd done even though I'd only been trying to protect them. They've been so good to me and I don't like seeing them upset.'

'I quite understand.'

'You're going to tell them about the envelope, aren't you?'

'I feel it's my duty to inform them. If I do then I'll be sure to stress that you removed it with the best of intentions.'

Fleming opened the envelope. As before, inside was a folded piece of paper. It too had only one word written on it: TRUTH. As before the envelope also contained a single item. This time it was a dried wild flower.

BACK IN HIS room Fleming had written his notes, freshened up, and changed for dinner. Having wound his pocket watch and slipped it into his waistcoat he looked for his precious tin. He'd asked the doctor to place it on the bedside table and not seeing it there he checked the drawer then hunted around the room. His heart-rate now galloping, he marched downstairs to find the doctor.

'I most certainly left it on the bedside table,' said Dr Ingrey. 'I did exactly as you asked.'

'You followed my instructions to the letter?'

'You have my word. We must do something. I know how much that tin means to you.'

'It was a parting gift from someone dear to me. However, it was my own foolishness that led to its loss, I should never have let it out of my sight. I'll inform reception, of course, but let's not allow its disappearance to spoil our evening meal.' Fleming led the way and Dr Ingrey followed. 'Cheer up, my friend, this was not your fault. Any culpability falls squarely at the feet of our thief.'

CHAPTER NINETEEN

TEDDY BEARS ALL

T he hotel's garden courtyard was blissfully cool and wooden seats were dotted here and there around the fountain trickling at its heart. Potted vines, olive, fig and citrus trees added fragrance, shade and colour.

Elsie was giddy with excitement. 'Answer Mr Fleming's question. What's the matter with you? You're acting like a man with a guilty conscience.' As she tilted her head with curiosity, her curly hair fell to one side. 'Forgive him, Mr Fleming, my little Teddy is as harmless as a mouse. He's simply one of those with a nervous disposition. Aren't you, darling?' She gave Teddy's arm a squeeze.

'Would you give me a moment, Elsie, please? You're always so loud. You don't give a man a chance to think. I simply can't concentrate with your incessant chattering.'

'Oh, I see! It's my fault you're unable to answer a simple question, is it? Rather more to the point, perhaps you shouldn't stay up drinking into the early hours?' She tried to put on a brave face but her cheeks were quite flushed.

'Would you repeat the question, Mr Fleming? I've lost my train of thought.' He looked between Fleming and Dr Ingrey.

'I asked whether your father is General Archibald Kelleher. The only reason I ask is that if he is your father then I met him once at a royal banquet in Windsor Castle.'

'I didn't know your father had met the King. Why on earth didn't you tell me?' squealed Elsie. She clapped her hands with delight and rocked back and forth in her chair. 'I'd love to meet anyone of the royal family, but particularly the King.'

Teddy raised his voice to make sure he was heard over Elsie. 'Yes, that would have been my father. The Grand Ol' Duke as I lovingly call him.'

'He's such an imposing looking gentleman,' said Elsie. 'He makes me quake in my boots when he speaks. He's so commanding and his voice booms. I almost want to salute each time he asks me a question!' said Elsie.

'You do go on, Elsie. He's just an ordinary fellow who thinks he's better than the rest of us just because he has a few medals almost permanently attached to his chest. I'm certain he'd sleep with them pinned to his pyjamas if he could.'

'Do I sense that you and he don't see eye to eye?' said Dr Ingrey.

'I'm what you might call a disappointment to him. My military career wasn't as glorious as his own. Let's just say I didn't distinguish myself in the heat of battle. It seems I'm not cut from same cloth as my father, the *inimitable* General Kelleher,' he added sarcastically.

'Your father is a man who struggles to show his feelings,' said Elsie sympathetically. 'I'm sure he's fond of you in his own way.'

'Oh, he's fond of me all right. I just come quite a way down the pecking order, somewhere between his dog and his walking boots.'

'I'm sure that's not true at all,' said Elsie reassuringly.

Teddy stared at his shoes for a moment before looking up and pursing his lips. 'It no longer matters to me what he thinks. Elsie understands, and together we've made our own life.'

Elsie took his hand and kissed it. 'We're quite the team, aren't we?'

Teddy gave her a wink. He then turned back to

Fleming. 'What on earth does my father have to do with poor Durante's death?'

'They say an apple never falls far from the tree, so I was curious to know whether you were indeed the son of General Kelleher,' said Fleming.

Teddy threw back his head and laughed. 'I understand it all now. You don't see eye to eye with my father and you were wondering whether I'm a bad apple just like him.'

'I've heard several first-hand accounts of his rather unflinching methods of discipline both on and off the battlefield.'

'The man is a throwback to the last century. I've heard those stories too and if I were you I'd believe every last word. They don't surprise me at all,' said Teddy. 'I'm not my father. It's why I stay as far away from him as I can.'

'I'm somewhat relieved to hear it,' said Fleming.

'I admit that from what I've seen you're a genial sort of fellow,' said Dr Ingrey. 'What was your opinion of Durante?'

'In truth, I don't have an opinion either way,' said Teddy. 'On the rare occasion we conversed I considered him a decent sort. I rather liked him. One had to forgive some of his more romantic views of the world, of course. I think his Italian nature made him a little too optimistic. Then again, maybe we British are too pessimistic? Who knows! That's a debate for another day, I suppose. All in all he was a friendly and charming bloke.'

Elsie agreed. 'He was a real darling to me but for the most part he very much kept himself to himself. I only chatted with him once or twice.'

'What sort of topics did you discuss?'

'He was interested in England. He had a fascination with King George,' said Teddy.

'He also wanted to know how well we knew the other guests,' added Elsie.

'Anyone in particular?'

'Not really,' said Teddy. 'He asked about Captain Maitland and his injury. He asked what type of doctor Ingrey was. He teased about Sir Ernest being a sir. He jokingly asked whether he lived in Camelot, wore a suit of armour like knights of old, and whether he sat at a round table like King Arthur and his knights.'

'I think he was interested in our English culture. He was very inquisitive.'

'Of course we had no idea he was a retired police inspector.'

'Looking back do you think he was interested in anyone in particular?'

The pair briefly looked at each other then shook their heads. 'No. I don't think so. He asked about everyone. Even you.'

'Me?'

'Yes. The first time we met him he asked if we knew you, and whether we thought it was odd that you spent so much time with Sir Ernest and Lady Templeton,' said Elsie.

'In truth, we hadn't really noticed,' admitted Teddy. 'We were getting on with our holiday. It wasn't until recently when we heard of Sir Ernest's trouble that we put two and two together and realised you were assisting him.'

Fleming leaned forward. 'On the night of his death some guests believe they heard somebody leave his room. Did you hear anything out of the ordinary that night?'

'No. We slept through,' said Elsie. 'The first we heard of it was when the body was discovered and young Rossi, the porter, appeared at the front desk all flustered. It was then that word quickly spread through the hotel.'

'Everyone was in shock, of course. Dolores was particularly distraught. Gerardo sat with her and comforted her. Even though he himself was white as a sheet,' said Elsie.

'That's quite true, she was surprisingly upset by the whole affair,' said Dr Ingrey. 'I talked to her, gave her a mild sedative, and ordered some hot sweet tea to steady her nerves. Lady Templeton eventually took over from Gerardo and Dolores appeared to settle soon after.'

'The *dotty pair* as I call them, Fern and Nancy, acted even more potty than usual. Fern behaved as though it were an everyday occurrence while Nancy was positively skittish.'

'One last thing for the moment,' said Fleming. He turned to Elsie. 'I've been meaning to ask whether you ever found your missing brooch?'

She was crestfallen. 'Sadly not. I've looked everywhere. It's the strangest thing. Out of all the items that could have been taken it had to be my brooch. It wasn't particularly valuable but was packed with sentimental value, of course, but isn't that always the way? Strangely, had they taken one of the more valuable pieces I'd have been happier.'

Dr Ingrey's eyes flicked towards Fleming. He wondered what was going through his mind. It was obvious how much sentimental value the great detective attached to the small ornate tin that he filled with sweet treats.

'I hope we were useful to your investigation,' said Teddy. 'It does seem as though that fellow Trotta was correct. I know he appears as if he's just fallen out of bed, I'm not sure he even bothers to brush his hair, but maybe appearances are deceptive. What do you say, Mr Fleming?'

Elsie's doe-like eyes widened. 'I must admit, I think Teddy has a point. After all, I can't see why any of the guests would have done him in. It's not as if any of us even met the chap before checking in to the hotel. Why would anyone wish him harm?'

'That's the type of question that's been keeping me awake at night, Mrs Kelleher. It's like a jigsaw puzzle, and all the pieces are jumbled up in this brain of mine. They're floating around, while I try to figure out what the finished picture should look like. At this point however, all I can do is ask my questions and attempt to try to understand where each piece fits.'

Over Teddy's shoulder Fleming caught a glimpse of Gerardo Castelli as he headed to the bar. He and the doctor thanked the Kellehers for their time and excused themselves.

Fleming took out his pocket watch and checked the time. 'It's late, why don't you retire for the evening?'

'Don't you require my assistance for our last interview of the day?'

Fleming kept an eye on Gerardo who now sat on the bar's open terrace nursing his drink. 'I have a feeling that young Gerardo will be more likely to open up if he doesn't feel cornered by the two of us. I think I should do this one alone.'

'Of course. You're quite right,' said Dr Ingrey. 'I'll make myself scarce.'

'Thank you, Doctor. I value your assistance. I'll bring you up to date in due course.'

The doctor retreated to the small taverna a short distance from the hotel and the attentions of the handsome widow who ran it.

CHAPTER TWENTY

O'ER VALES AND HILLS

Placing his mint tea on the table, Fleming sat alongside Gerardo. The young man looked up from his book; it was worn and tattered and an attempt had been made to fix the spine.

Fleming began: 'I wandered lonely as a Cloud,

That floats on high o'er Vales and Hills.'

Gerardo continued: 'When all at once I saw a crowd,

A host of golden Daffodils;

Beside the Lake, beneath the trees,

Fluttering and dancing in the breeze.'

Fleming chuckled. 'You're a fan of William Wordsworth?'

'I have precious little that belonged to my mother, but this book, and other books of poetry are some of the few items that remain. When I read them I feel like they bring me closer to her. I want to share in something she enjoyed. I think it would have made her happy.' He closed the book and put it down on the table. 'I wondered when you'd finally get around to questioning me.'

'For a little while I got the feeling you were avoiding me. Yet, this evening I find you waiting to talk to me. I'll admit, I'm more than a little intrigued.'

'I'm sure I'm not the only one who's been avoiding you, Mr Fleming. Who in their right mind wants to be interrogated about murder?'

'You make a good point. Nevertheless, I must ask you again about the incident I observed. The altercation between you and Durante. You both appeared quite angry. And please don't insult my intelligence by suggesting it was nothing. The angry exchange was intense and passionate.'

'I thought he was a criminal. Maybe the person who had been stealing from the hotel's guests. He had this air about him that I was uncertain of. It was as if he was always watching and snooping. I took a dislike to him. That day you saw us arguing I realised he was following me. I'd seen him several times at the same places I'd visited, and when I eventually observed him watching me I confronted him. He didn't like that. He denied following me. I didn't believe him.'

Fleming frowned. 'At the opera you gave me a

different account. You told me that Durante had shared his unwelcome opinion on your interest in Dolores, and that was why you'd argued.'

Gerardo rolled his neck. 'I didn't feel it appropriate to blacken the man's character without hard evidence, so I said the first thing that came to mind. Just as well under the circumstances.'

'At the time you had no idea he was a retired policeman?'

'I had no idea. I found out at the same time as the rest of the guests. It now makes me wonder whether he was following not just me, but other guests as well. Maybe whatever he was looking for led to his untimely death.'

'I'll admit I've been wondering the same thing.' Fleming sipped his mint tea. 'You're quite certain you've never met him until your arrival at this hotel?'

'I'm positive.'

'You've seen him following other guests.'

'Not only that, but I once caught him reading the hotel's guest register. He pretended he wasn't but I know what I saw.'

'That's interesting,' said Fleming.

'It occurred to me that perhaps he wasn't actually interested in any of the current guests but was in fact investigating someone who had been at the hotel before we arrived. Or maybe, he was on the wrong track and it's a case of mistaken identity.'

'That wouldn't, I think, account for someone who is currently staying at the hotel ending his life.'

Gerardo looked disappointed. 'Of course. How stupid of me. You feel certain then that his killer is a current guest?'

'I have no doubt whatsoever.' Fleming glanced at the book of poetry. 'Was your mother fond of English poets in particular?'

'From what I understand she had planned to move to England.'

'She fell in love?'

Gerardo's eyes narrowed.

Fleming rephrased: 'She fell in love with the country?'

'I'm told that when I was a baby she would sing to me and tell me stories in both English and my native tongue. She was an incredibly intelligent woman. Her father, my grandfather, was a wealthy landowner, and local politician.'

'And what of your father?'

'He was also a wealthy man. Though I never really knew him. The truth is, after my mother passed away he abandoned me.'

'I'm sorry. That can be hard on a child.'

'There are far worse things that can happen to a child, than an uncaring father.'

'You're correct, of course. I've encountered many tragic stories. Too often they lead to further tragedies later in life. I'm glad to see that you've suffered no such impediment.'

'On the contrary. I have fond memories of my childhood, with many friends and family around me. I had what you'd call a privileged upbringing. My grandfather, whom I love dearly, is frail and I'll soon inherit part of his vast fortune, and his estate.'

'Yet, you're here in Venice alone?'

'Before the estate passes to me, along with all its many responsibilities, I want to travel the length of my homeland. I'm a proud Italian, and I wish to know my magnificent country better, as well as the troubles of my fellow countrymen.'

'A fine idea. Knowing where one comes from is a worthy endeavour.' Fleming finished his tea and got to his feet. He gave a little bow and bid Gerardo goodnight. He reached the door and turned. 'As you might imagine, as a private investigator I meet many people from all walks of life. Rich, poor, happy, sad. Thankfully, most of them aren't guilty of any crime. Some of them are of course the victims of crime. And the crimes perpetrated against them vary hugely in seriousness. I've seen enough victims to come to recognise a look in their eye.'

'What do you say to those people?'

'It varies, but I'll usually caution them that dwelling too long on the darkness of the past might well overshadow any chance of a bright future.'

'Fortunately, I'm well aware that my future is what I make it. Whether that's for better or for worse.' He picked up his book of poetry and opened it once more. 'Goodnight, Mr Fleming.'

Captain Maitland stepped aside and pointed to the door which was damaged close to the lock. 'You might want to take a look at this, Mr Fleming.'

Fleming was passing the captain's room on the way to his own to retire for the night.

'What appears to be the problem?'

'It's this.' The door and frame were dented and splintered. 'The thing's been forced open.'

The two men entered the captain's room and looked around.

'I'd already checked before you came along and I can't say I've noticed that anything's missing. Then again, I don't have anything of any real value anyway. In truth I'm an odd choice for any thief to consider.'

Fleming's eyes appraised the room. There were very few personal effects on display. The room remained neat and tidy. No drawers or cupboard doors were open the way they might be if a thief had rifled through them.

'The room is how you left it?' asked Fleming.

'I think so.' He absently pushed closed the bureau drawer that was slightly open. 'As I say I have no valuables, or large sums of cash in the room.' He chuckled at the idea.

'The drawer you just closed. What's kept in there?'

Captain Maitland frowned and looked at the drawer. 'Only writing paper. A letter I started and can't seem to finish.'

Fleming opened the drawer.

'Oh, and my journal,' said Captain Maitland lifting it out. 'It mostly consists of my personal ramblings.' He pushed the journal to the back of the drawer and slid the drawer shut. 'I usually keep the bureau drawers locked, I must have forgotten.'

'Let me guess,' said Fleming, 'the key is hidden on top of the wardrobe?'

Captain Maitland reached up on top of the wardrobe, his hand feeling around for the cold metal. 'Here it is. How did you know I'd keep it there?' he asked while locking the drawer.

'It's a most common and obvious hiding place,'

said Fleming. 'If nothing was stolen you must consider yourself lucky. Either our little magpie discovered no glittering jewels and simply flew away, or they were disturbed and made a hasty retreat.'

'Our hotel thief picked the wrong target on this occasion.'

'You might be right.' Fleming had an odd look on his face. 'It's curious to me that our hotel thief should force the door like that. Until now they've entered each room with apparent ease and with no damage caused.' He waved his musings away. 'Let's not unnecessarily expend energies on a matter of little consequence. Have you informed the reception manageress of the intrusion and damage to the door?'

'I had better do that now.'

'In which case, if you no longer require my assistance, I'll bid you good night. My mind is in need of its rest.' Fleming gave a slight nod and went to his room.

Despite the impression he might have given Captain Maitland that the break-in was of little concern, he lay awake for some considerable time contemplating the incident before finally drifting off to sleep.

PART III

BUT, IN THE END, TRUTH WILL OUT

CHAPTER TWENTY-ONE

CONFINED TO BARRACKS

As Fleming entered the dining room there was a hush amongst the guests. He bid everyone good morning and waited for his breakfast: two boiled eggs, fresh bread, and a pot of tea. While he sat and read his newspaper he noticed a glance first from Sir Ernest, then in turn from Nancy, Fern, Teddy and Elsie. He folded his newspaper and put it down.

Captain Maitland was sitting at the same table as Dr Ingrey. The two of them looked over.

Fleming frowned. 'Am I missing something, Captain Maitland?'

'You don't know?' said Dr Ingrey.

'Know what?'

'Gerardo has gone. He packed his things in the middle of the night and fled the hotel.'

'Obviously a guilty conscience,' said Lady Templeton.

'Fleeing the scene of the crime,' added Fern. 'Only a criminal would do that.'

'What are you going to do about it?' asked Teddy. 'Will you inform Inspector Trotta?'

'I'm fully aware of the situation,' said Fleming. His eggs and bread arrived. He thanked the waiter and set about attacking the shell of his eggs with the back of his spoon. He buttered and cut his bread into soldiers and began dipping them into the warm orangey goo.

Voices in the room grew louder as the guests questioned what should be done.

'Surely, you're going to have him arrested?'

'He should face justice for what he's done. A good man is dead.'

'He can't be allowed to roam free.'

'What if he does it again?'

'Some other poor soul murdered in their bed.'

The voices grew louder and more insistent.

Fleming put down his spoon, rose to his feet and tapped his knife against the side of a glass with a *clank! clank! clank!* The sharp noise cut through the din. Everyone fell silent. All eyes turned to Fleming.

'Ladies and gentlemen, I am of course aware that Signor Gerardo Castelli has left us. In fact, I was notified in the early hours by the porter, Signor Rossi. I had made the request of both he and Signorina Lombardi that I should be informed immediately should any guest attempt to leave.'

There were murmurs of discontent.

'You deliberately let him go?' said Sir Ernest.

As he spoke Fleming looked at every guest in turn. 'Gerardo remains a suspect. However, at this time I saw no good reason to detain him further. I assure you, I will be speaking to him again. I plan to travel to his home in the next few days.'

'That seems rather rich considering we're still confined to barracks,' said Captain Maitland. 'I'm aware I'm exaggerating but it's rather unpleasant having this investigation hanging over us day and night.'

'This will all be over soon, you have my word,' said Fleming.

'When? When will it be over?' asked Lady Templeton. 'I think it's high time we had some answers.'

'I'd certainly like to know the truth,' said Elsie. 'It was all quite thrilling at first but I'm starting to feel quite down about it.'

'Give me a few more hours and I'll reveal all,' said Fleming.

The room once again filled with excited voices as Fleming returned to his breakfast.

Dr Ingrey pulled up a chair beside him. 'Have you really figured out who murdered Durante?'

Fleming took a pinch of salt and sprinkled a little into his second soft boiled egg. 'The motivation for the murder eluded me for quite some time but I'm pleased to say that last night I had an epiphany. Today I have contacted Inspector Trotta and shortly I'll expect confirmation of my theory. If I'm correct, which I have little doubt I am, then tomorrow I shall present my findings.'

'Well I never.' The doctor tried to swallow, his throat suddenly dry. 'I'd better leave you to your breakfast. I think I'll take a walk. If you need me I'll be back around midday.'

Fleming smoothed fruit preserve onto his last remaining piece of crusty bread. 'Enjoy your walk, Doctor.'

THE SMELL of the finely woven wool filled his nostrils. The fabric was smooth and soft to the touch. Fleming looked in the mirror. He turned, first left, then right. He held his arms out in front of him and checked the length of the sleeves, considered how it felt under the arms.

The tailor, a small man with deep creases across his

forehead, and fingers that moved as deftly as a concert pianist's, ran his hand over the jacket's shoulders, then down the back, his eyes taking in every line and seam. He knelt and adjusted the fall of the trousers.

'*Perfezione*,' he said, rising to his full height, which was no more than Fleming's shoulder. 'What do you think?'

'I agree. It's perfect. You're a maestro, signor.'

The old man's eyes shone. His body gently rocked from side to side with delight. 'When I tell my wife that you are my newest customer, she did not believe me. I tell her that it's true. He came to my little shop. Nobody else's shop in the whole of Italy, he came to mine. Signor Henry Fleming of England wants one of my suits for his investigation.' He proudly thrust out his chin. 'Please understand, I love her with the depth of the deepest ocean, and far beyond the height of any mountain. She is my sun and my moon, but do you know what she said to me?'

Fleming shook his head.

'She tells me that I'm going mad to the head. She says the sun has finally turned my brain to sand. *Incredibile!* Can you believe it?' He held up a calling card that Fleming had given him. 'Here is my proof. Now she has to believe me!'

The old tailor's eyes returned to the suit. He carefully lifted the jacket from Fleming's shoulders. 'If the suit is to your satisfaction I will have it delivered to your hotel this afternoon.'

'That would be ideal,' said Fleming. 'Mr Buford, of Buford and Doyle, my London tailor, wasn't wrong in his recommendation. I shall wear this suit with the utmost pride.'

'The pleasure is most certainly all mine, Signor Fleming.'

Fleming left the tailor's and took a long walk. Aware his time in Venice would soon be coming to an end he retraced his steps around the city, visiting several of his favourite places. Committing the sights, sounds, smells and tastes to memory.

'It is you, Mr Fleming!' exclaimed Captain Maitland. He leaned on his walking stick. 'I assume that just like me you needed to get as far from that hotel as possible. It feels tainted since Durante's death.'

'I hadn't thought of it that way but perhaps my outlook on such matters is a little different to that of others.'

Captain Maitland adjusted the brim of his hat. 'Perhaps.'

The two men began walking. Fleming matching the captain's slow pace.

'I've been wondering, Fleming. How did a man like you get into all this business of... detecting?' He attempted to gauge how the detective felt about this question but saw no flicker of unease.

'A man like me?'

'I mean, you're an educated man, I'm sure you could have risen to the top of almost any profession. You clearly have many influential friends who I'm sure have offered you positions over the years. Why spend your time rifling through other people's laundry?'

'Their laundry?' chuckled Fleming.

'You know what I mean. Don't you get tired of uncovering so much wickedness? I'm not sure I could stomach hearing about all the betrayals, greed, envy, hatred, affairs, and lies.'

'When it comes to human nature, which is something about my work that fascinates me, those are but one side of the coin. Those behaviours are far from tiresome. Something you might find equally interesting is that a crime may be committed just as readily over love, friendship, hope, honesty, and truth.'

'I hadn't thought of it that way. I suppose you're right.'

'What about you, Captain Maitland? You've mentioned teaching. Was that simply said to stave off my questions, or was there some truth behind it?'

'As soon as I return I'll be seeking a teaching position in some remote corner of England.'

'Most wise.'

Captain Maitland took this to mean he approved of the decision to be far from Elsie. 'And of course, it's imperative she never knows how I *really* feel about her.'

'I must stop you there. You act as though these feelings you mention are one-sided. I see with certainty that they're not. In front of Dr Ingrey I allowed you to suggest unchallenged that that was the case, but the truth is I have little doubt she once had feelings for you too. I can only assume that at one time there was romance between you.'

'I've loved her since the day we met. Before the war I'd considered proposing to her. I hesitated, and when I returned she and Teddy...'

'I'm sorry.'

'There's nothing to be sorry about. Look at me.' He held up his walking cane. 'She's better off with Teddy and I've told her as much.'

Fleming came to an abrupt halt. 'You're not being entirely truthful with me. You're trying to protect Elsie's honour and that's most valiant, however, if you and she have expressed feelings for each other more recently then you're playing with fire!'

Captain Maitland paled. 'The truth is, I've hinted to her about my feelings for her. I don't know whether she actually feels as strongly about me. I don't think she realises how she makes me feel when I'm around her. Especially as she's a naturally flirtatious kind of girl. I'm not sure she knows she's doing it. When I'm with her I lose my mind.' He sighed. 'It's important I get away. Far, far away.'

'Since she's been married have you and she ever...?'

'Goodness me, no! I can't say I haven't thought about it. Most nights I drink to excess to block the thought. One day I want to be able to close my eyes and not see her face, her smile, her lips before I sleep. I know some of the guests assume she and I have been intimate behind Teddy's back but you have my word, as a gentleman, that despite my feelings for her, nothing has happened. As you've suggested, it would be disastrous.'

'A disaster of the highest magnitude!'

'You're right, of course.'

'Shall we stop at this café for a while?' said Fleming, seeing Captain Maitland's discomfort.

'You go ahead. I'll rest a while. I don't wish to hold you up.'

'You're not holding me up.'

'No, no, please go ahead. I need some time alone.'

'If you insist,' said Fleming.

'I do. I'll see you back at the hotel later.'

Fleming took his time and walked for another hour until he eventually circled back to where he'd left Captain Maitland. From a distance he noticed Elsie sitting alone at a small table. She got to her feet and was about to leave when from inside the café appeared Captain Maitland. They embraced and she laughed as he whispered in her ear. The pair then parted, her hand lingering momentarily in the air as they went their separate ways.

Fleming let out a heavy sigh. 'So many lies and such stupidity!'

As Elsie came his way, Fleming hastily turned and entered the nearest small shop which, much to his dismay, he discovered was selling ladies' lingerie. Too late to rectify his blunder, and under the clearly suspicious gaze of the shop assistant, he pretended to browse. As soon as Elsie had passed, he bid the assistant an embarrassed but polite farewell and exited as quickly as he'd entered.

CHAPTER TWENTY-TWO

THE TRUTH OF SWALLOWBARN HALL

F leming had shut himself away in his room and refused to see or speak to anyone. He paced back and forth in his undergarments, shirt and socks. His mind was in such turmoil that even focusing on the simple act of dressing for dinner had become a challenge.

The additional information he'd requested from Inspector Trotta regarding Gerardo sat neatly on his writing bureau. It had been hand-delivered shortly after lunch and it confirmed his worst fears.

This evening he would unmask Durante's killer. Inspector Trotta had agreed on the telephone that he should be granted the opportunity to expose the truth and at the appropriate time Trotta himself would make the arrest. It was apparent Trotta was curious about the outcome. If only, perhaps, to see Fleming with egg on his face should things go wrong.

Fleming had sent a telegram to Gerardo in the hope he would attend this evening's *grande rivelazione* but he held out little hope he'd show his face. Instead he anticipated a need to confront him at a later date.

Fleming opened his wardrobe and took out his newly tailored Italian wool three-piece suit. He dressed, then carefully removed a few stray threads, brushed away a small piece of fluff from the pin-striped navy blue material. He examined his shoes which had been freshly polished to a mirror finish by Arturo. 'Perfect,' he said.

His heart sank as he put a flat hand to the bespoke inside pocket where he usually kept his ornate tin filled with sugary treats. He picked up his pocket watch and allowed his eyes to linger on the portrait of the woman he kept inside the case. He took a moment to remember her. Fixing the pocket-watch chain he gently slipped the timepiece into his waistcoat. He took a long calming breath and headed downstairs to the waiting guests. Halfway down, on the second landing, he was met by Dr Ingrey.

'Are you ready, Doctor?' said Fleming.

'As I'll ever be.'

The two men entered the dining room together

and the room instantly fell silent. 'If everyone would take their seats, we'll begin,' commanded Fleming.

Sir Ernest downed a brandy, quickly followed by another. Arm in arm Lady Templeton and Dolores took seats together. Elsie held out two glasses while Teddy poured champagne for them both. Captain Maitland stood alone at the edge of the room beside a door that opened onto the terrace. He took his time finishing his cigarette, tossed the butt then, collecting his glass of gin, took his place at the table.

Fern and Nancy were whispering in a corner. They shuffled into the centre of the room, mumbling apologies, and causing commotion as they unnecessarily moved two seats closer together. Fern stared wide-eyed at the other guests while Nancy sat clutching her handbag.

Receptionist Signorina Lombardi and Signor Rossi the hotel porter sat side by side at the table.

Fleming remained standing and at his behest Dr Ingrey sat to his left.

The one empty seat at the end of the table belonged to Gerardo.

Elsie whispered to Teddy. 'I have to admit, this is all quite stirring.'

Teddy raised his eyebrows. 'It's only stirring until you find yourself wrongly accused by this puffed-up know-it-all. It's not going to seem as thrilling if you find Trotta marching you off to some stinking dungeon! The thing to remember is that this fellow has no authority. If he accuses me, or you, we're buying the first ticket out of this city.'

Overhearing their conversation Fern shuddered.

'Don't worry, Fern,' said Elsie. 'He can be a little overdramatic. I'm sure nobody here will be thrown into a dungeon.'

Teddy pulled a face that suggested he wasn't so sure.

Sir Ernest raised a steadying hand. 'I think that's quite enough of that talk, Mr Kelleher. You're scaring the womenfolk. Let's hear what the chap has to say. After all, the only reason he's standing in front of us now is because my wife, in her wisdom, paid the man a small fortune to be here.'

Fleming waited for silence. 'I assume everyone is aware of the fact, but in case there's any doubt we have one guest who it's unlikely will be joining us. Gerardo Castelli departed last night. This was against my wishes and, in my opinion, his decision reflects poorly on his character. I would have appreciated his presence as I explain what led to the murderous act inflicted upon our fellow guest Signor Antonio Durante.'

Captain Maitland moved his chair closer to the open terrace door. 'I need another smoke. It seems pretty obvious to me Gerardo killed Durante for reasons unknown and absconded. I don't see why we need to be here. Let's face it, Fleming, your suspect escaped. He's probably hiding in some obscure little place up in the mountains, or a fishing village tucked away in some small cove. You should have hooked your fish when you had your chance. Instead, he's slipped through your fingers.'

Fleming frowned. 'Gerardo is guilty.'

'What?' said Lady Templeton.

'I know exactly what he's done.'

'You do? Then why on earth didn't you say so,' chuckled Sir Ernest. 'That's wonderful news. I take it all back, Fleming, you're a genius. Just like they claim you are.'

'I must admit,' said Nancy. 'I never would have guessed. He seemed like a lovely young man to me. Very handsome. Lovely skin.'

'Now's not the time, Nancy,' said Fern. 'Though I must admit, his complexion did look remarkably smooth, especially for a killer.'

Fleming raised his voice. 'Let me be clear. Gerardo *is* guilty of a crime. However, that crime isn't murder. I repeat. He did *not* kill Durante.'

Dr Ingrey scratched his head. 'Are you saying there are two crimes?'

'In fact, Doctor, there are at least four crimes. We will get to each of them in turn.'

'Good heavens!' exclaimed Dr Ingrey. 'Well I never.'

'This complex state of affairs began long before Lady Templeton invited me to extend my stay here in Venice and which ultimately led to Durante's death. It was Lady Templeton who tasked me with uncovering the identity of the intruder at Swallowbarn Hall. Described as a devil-like figure, that watched from afar and had menacing intentions. Who is also now suspected of leaving sinister notes and tokens addressed to Sir Ernest. It's this same mysterious visitor who was involved in the diamond necklace stolen from the safe in Sir Ernest's study on the night of the break-in.'

'It's worth a tidy sum,' Lady Templeton informed the room. She took Sir Ernest's hand. 'It was my mother-in-law's. An antique that passed to me on our wedding day and had been passed to her on her wedding day. Exquisite Russian diamonds.'

'Insured of course,' explained Sir Ernest. 'It's not until an item of such value is gone that you realise that the money pales into insignificance when compared to the sentimental value. It was one of a kind.'

'An insurance payout cannot, of course, replace the irreplaceable,' said Fleming.

'The money is no substitute for something so precious,' explained Lady Templeton. 'Fortunately, we're extremely financially sound. Aren't we, Ernest?'

'Extremely financially sound,' echoed Sir Ernest.

'In that case only one explanation exists, does it not? Someone else in the household stole the necklace.'

'I explained to you, Mr Fleming,' said Lady Templeton, 'that the mysterious Professor Bonnard must have stolen the necklace when he broke in. This person knew it was of great value to Sir Ernest and would therefore hurt him deeply. He then began sending the sickening notes. It simply has to be the same person.'

'That's as may be, Lady Templeton, but I know the identity of the mysterious Professor Bonnard and this person could not have stolen the necklace. Professor Bonnard certainly broke into Swallowbarn Hall, however it wasn't the diamond necklace he was looking for.'

'I don't understand,' said Lady Templeton, imperiously raising her head. 'I hired you to find out who was intimidating my husband.'

'I've done better than that. I found your Professor Bonnard, the thief, and the diamond necklace.'

'You've what?!' she blurted, her eyes suddenly ice cold. 'That is *not* what I asked you to do.'

Fleming continued. 'You see the necklace was sold to a rather unscrupulous jewellery dealer in North London three days *before* the break-in. I sent a telegram to my good friend, Inspector Carp at Scotland Yard requesting his assistance, and it didn't take long for him to track down this dealer, and for him to hand over the necklace which he claims to have purchased in good faith.'

Lady Templeton's voice trembled. 'I'm so relieved to hear the necklace has been recovered. I suppose the mysterious visitor is long gone?'

'Timing is everything in situations of this nature and I've established that it would have been impossible for the mysterious Professor Bonnard to have stolen the diamond necklace.'

'You're wrong,' said Dolores suddenly, her face full of panic. 'It was taken by Professor Bonnard, it has to have been.'

Fleming pressed on. 'Inspector Carp recovered the necklace, which fortunately had not yet been dismantled and sold in pieces as is the most common way with jewellery of such provenance. When questioned about who brought in the necklace, the dealer described a dark-haired woman, similar in stature and appearance to Dolores.'

Dolores gasped. She was about to speak when Lady Templeton raised a hand to silence her.

'That's absurd,' said Lady Templeton. 'For a start, Dolores's hair is red, not dark.'

'Easily remedied with a wig. He also mentioned identifying scars.'

Dolores instinctively moved her hands onto her lap and out of sight.

'Though the woman wore gloves he happened to glimpse scarring above her wrist. Would you care to show me your scars?' said Fleming.

'There's no need,' said Lady Templeton. Her lips were pinched tight. 'I made her do it.'

'You're admitting your part in selling the necklace and claiming the insurance money?'

'Dolores had no choice. She was unaware of my intentions. I told her that I'd arranged for a man to buy the necklace and she must take it to him. I bought her a wig to hide her identity. I told her I was concerned if she was seen there might be talk of my selling it, and gossip surrounding our financial situation. In the beginning, I had no intention of claiming the insurance. However, by some stroke of good fortune when the break-in occurred I saw an opportunity; it suddenly became useful. Afterwards, I simply informed the police the necklace had been stolen. I then insisted Dolores play along with my story. If she didn't, both she and I would most certainly land ourselves in trouble with the law.'

Sir Ernest, who had been silent throughout the proceedings, suddenly found his voice. 'But why? Our financial situation isn't as dire as all that.'

'My dear sweet Ernest, you live far beyond your

means. You always have. No matter how much money you make you find a way to spend it. This trip is a case in point. It's a glorious and perfect example of your generosity but a drain on our already challenged finances. I decided I needed some capital of my own in case the worst should happen.' She put a loving hand on his chest. 'Your health is no longer what it was. I was worried beyond words I might lose you and I did something very silly, and quite out of character.'

Fleming turned to Dolores. 'Your part in this affair is questionable. It's quite possible you were unaware of Lady Templeton's deceptions. However, you disguised yourself and took the necklace to a shady London jewel dealer. You then actively played a part in lying to the police, and to me, about the matters surrounding the break-in and theft at Swallowbarn Hall. Whether pressures were placed upon you by Lady Templeton, or whether you were a willing participant, I cannot say for certain. That comes down to Lady Templeton's word on the matter. It has made me wonder whether the guilt of your misplaced loyalty is the real reason behind your ambitions to travel and get away from Swallowbarn Hall.'

Dolores lowered her gaze, unable to look at either Fleming or Lady Templeton. She spoke in a whisper. 'It was exciting at first. I wanted to please Lady Templeton, and help Sir Ernest. It all got out of hand

and was quickly more than I agreed to but I felt trapped. I didn't know what to do. I'm sorry, Mr Fleming.' Large, fat tears began to roll slowly down her cheeks.

'We'll return to the matter of the mystery man, Professor Bonnard, and the sinister letters shortly.' Fleming turned his attention to Dr Ingrey who was watching with fascination. His eyes widened when he saw Fleming looking at him. 'First, there is something else that we must explore,' said Fleming.

CHAPTER TWENTY-THREE

LIGHT-FINGERED FRIENDS

Fleming placed his hand over the bespoke jacket pocket. 'I usually carry an ornate tin in here that's incredibly precious to me. However, it's gone missing from my room. It was originally filled with sweet treats and given to me by someone I loved dearly. I've continued the tradition of filling the tin and carrying it with me wherever I go as a reminder of her. This gift was stolen from my bedside table.

'As we all know I'm not the only one to have had items removed from their room. Items of value, whether that value is sentimental or monetary. At first I wondered whether the thefts here at the hotel were linked to the break-in at Swallowbarn Hall, but I soon realised they were not.

'Having spent some time watching staff, hotel visitors, and finally each guest, I came to the conclusion the thief, or thieves, knew the hotel well. They were able to move around freely and not be suspected of stealing from the rooms. I was confident the thief was not staff, or an outsider, but a guest. I decided the best way to proceed was to set a trap.'

Dr Ingrey's eyes widened as he realised his role in the trap. 'You had me deliberately leave your tin on display in your room knowing there was a strong possibility of it being taken.'

'I couldn't tell you of my plan as I required you to act naturally when mentioning during your conversation with guests that I wasn't in my room, that I would be engaged for some time with Sir Ernest and Lady Templeton in the reading room. Like the trusted beater on a big game hunt, I employed you to flush out our quarry.'

'You sly fox,' chuckled Dr Ingrey.

'And it worked!' said Fleming proudly.

'Well, don't keep me in suspense, old chap, who's our thief?'

'Why don't I allow Signorina Lombardi and Signor Rossi to tell you. I asked them to keep an eye on those visiting my room while I was with Sir Ernest and Lady Templeton.'

Signorina Lombardi and Signor Rossi got to their feet. Both appeared uncomfortable with Fleming's request to point out the thief in such a public manner.

Fleming looked to Signorina Lombardi. 'After I asked you to observe the guests and their movements did you see anything of interest?'

'I did,' said the signorina. Her face reddened. 'As instructed, I waited for Dr Ingrey to return your room key. That was my signal to note any guest who went upstairs to the rooms. I then signalled to our hotel porter,' she pointed to Signor Rossi, 'who like a spy observed their movements.'

Fleming turned to the porter. 'Please tell those gathered what you told me about a guest entering my room.'

The usually chatty porter was a little apprehensive. 'I watched as several guests used the stairs. I followed each one, pretending to be attending to my duties, all the while observing their movements as you instructed me, Mr Fleming. Eventually, I saw a guest entering a room which was not their own.'

'Whose room did they enter?'

'Yours, Mr Fleming.'

'How do you think they gained access?'

The porter scratched his head. 'I know for a fact Signorina Lombardi had your room key in her keeping. Dr Ingrey had given it to her for safekeeping.'

Signorina Lombardi nodded to acknowledge this to be true.

'How do you suppose they were able to enter my

room, Signor Rossi, without my room key?' repeated Fleming.

'They would need a...' Rossi paused. His hand went to his empty pocket.

Fleming knew exactly why he hesitated. 'They would need a master key like the one lifted from your pocket by our light-fingered thief. You didn't misplace your key; you were pick-pocketed by an experienced thief who knew exactly what they were doing.' Fleming moved around the table where the guests were seated. 'Who was it that you saw enter my room, Signor Rossi?'

The porter's eyes became accusatory. He raised his hand and pointed a finger.

Unable to follow all the talk, Nancy had become bored and taken up her knitting. At first she was unaware of the pointing finger. It wasn't until Fern nudged her that she looked up. 'What have I missed?' she asked, confused.

'It would appear you missed very little in your game of larceny,' said Fleming.

'Oh dear me, no,' said Fern. 'You have it all wrong. Nancy's a far too gentle and timid a soul to do such a thing.'

'Enough of this charade, please. You and I know the truth and it's time to make amends as best you can.' He turned once again to Rossi and the young porter briefly stepped outside only to return seconds later with a case the size of a doctor's medical bag. He handed it to Fleming who placed it on the table in front of everyone.

'That's like mine,' said Nancy. She looked again. 'It *is* mine. That's my private property!' She was outraged.

'Ironically, the contents of which are other people's property.' He unfastened the clip and reached inside. Piece by piece he placed the stolen items on the table for all to see.

'My brooch!' squealed Elsie.

'My powder compact,' said Dolores.

'Good lord!' said Captain Maitland. 'My cigarette case.'

Dolores also recognised the silver bracelet she had been accused of stealing by the angry Venetian shop owner.

Dr Ingrey got to his feet. He looked among the items then up at Fleming. 'I see Gerardo's wrist-watch, but there's no sign of your own precious sweet tin.'

'I must assume it hasn't yet been moved to this case and remains in the bag in which it was first placed.'

Nancy dropped her knitting and clasped her handbag for dear life.

Fleming put out a hand. 'I must insist you pass it to me, please.'

With Fern's encouragement Nancy released the crocodile leather bag.

Fleming unfastened it and looked inside. Having taken out her belongings there was still no sign of his tin. He pressed the sides of the bag, then examined it more closely. 'You informed me that this was especially made for you. One bespoke feature that you did not happen to mention was ... *voila!* ... a secret compartment.' He placed his precious decorated tin on the table alongside the porter's master key.

'My master key!' said Rossi, with relief. 'I didn't lose it. It was stolen!'

'Well I never!' said Dr Ingrey. 'You've uncovered a veritable treasure trove.'

Fleming held aloft the crocodile handbag to reveal a side pocket. 'You cleverly slipped the items you stole into this hidden pocket. Perfect concealment should you be stopped and questioned and your bag examined.'

'We meant no real harm,' said Fern. 'We sell the things to supplement our travelling. We learned that taking it in turns to procure the items, and not picking up high value objects, raised fewer suspicions. Most travellers assume they simply misplaced what we've taken. After all, they're travelling out of a suitcase and in unfamiliar surroundings. If they're convinced it was stolen, they're rarely able to pursue the complaint for long because they're typically only in the country a few weeks. Furthermore, local police really aren't interested in foreigners who grumble about the theft of low-worth items. Our little system has worked well until now.'

'Low worth to you, perhaps,' raged Elsie. 'This brooch means a lot to me.'

Nancy looked perturbed. 'Are we in a spot of bother, d'you think, Fern?' she asked.

'Well, it would seem we've been rumbled, dear,' said Fern.

'Does that mean we won't be travelling on through the rest of Italy? I so want to visit Rome, Fern.' Her eyes had filled with disappointed tears.

Fern gently patted her hand. 'Don't fret, Nance. We'll have to wait and see how inclined the Italian police force is to press charges against two little old English ladies. I've a feeling they've more important issues to deal with.'

'Oh, Fern, d'you think so? That's such a relief.'

'You carry on with your knitting and don't worry.' She turned to the other guests. 'She's not well, you know. I don't think an Italian prison cell is the best place for her.'

'You might have thought of that before indulging in such behaviour,' said Teddy pompously. 'I for one have little sympathy. I can't say I want to see you both

224

locked up but I do feel there needs to be some form of recompense. After all, where would we be without law and order?'

'Where indeed?' said Fleming. He stopped by Teddy and briefly placed a hand on his shoulder before continuing to walk slowly around the table to the front of the room.

'Why is everyone looking at me? I'm not guilty of anything,' blustered Teddy.

CHAPTER TWENTY-FOUR

LOVE TRIANGLE

Teddy Kelleher's face was fixed in a grimace.

When Fleming eventually turned his attention to Captain Maitland, Teddy appeared relieved. 'Yes, exactly, he's the one you need to question. Not me,' said Teddy. 'My so called friend – Judas more like!'

Captain Maitland got to his feet and walked to the table where all the stolen items sat. He leaned across and snatched up his cigarette case. He returned to his seat, snapped it open and took out a cigarette. Having lit it he turned to Teddy. 'You might be the only real friend I have in this world, but you're also a fool.'

'That might be true. I believed you'd never betray me but I was wrong.'

'How exactly did I do that?'

Teddy jumped to his feet and pointed an

accusatory finger at Maitland. 'It doesn't take a genius to realise you've been actively pursuing my wife. I pretend to turn a blind eye to it. I know Elsie wouldn't deceive me. I'm not a man who courts conflict but it's gone on long enough. I've seen your journal. The entries where you've declared your love for her.'

Captain Maitland fought hard to restrain his anger. 'How would you know what's in my journal, Teddy?'

Fleming intervened. 'There's only one way he could know, and that is if he entered your room and read it.'

Teddy's mouth opened and closed like a gasping fish. His eyes moved between Captain Maitland's, Fleming's, and Elsie's.

'Oh, Teddy,' said Elsie. She pouted with disappointment. 'You didn't, did you?'

'I had to be sure,' was all he could muster.

'You foolish man, you know I'd never betray you.' She took his hand and kissed it.

Teddy looked sheepish.

'At first I assumed the hotel thief had forced the lock to Captain Maitland's room. However, this didn't follow the usual pattern of theft where items are removed without any disturbance. Though Captain Maitland's cigarette case had gone missing he insisted it hadn't been left in his room, and so could not have been taken from there. This led me to believe that the cigarette case was taken at a different time, perhaps it was left unattended at the bar, in the dining room, or on the terrace, and our light-fingered friend seeing an opportunity snatched it up. As soon as I understood that Fern and Nancy were responsible for the thefts I knew with certainty they wouldn't have had the strength, or need, to force the lock to his room. We now know they had a master key. I then asked myself who else would so desperately want to get into the captain's room. I soon realised that a man who required the truth behind his worst fears would force a lock and cover it up.'

Teddy wiped away the perspiration that now covered his face and neck.

'It was you who forced the lock and entered Captain Maitland's room,' asserted Fleming.

'The jig's up,' said Captain Maitland. 'You might as well get it all off your chest. Otherwise, there's a chance you'll be pegged as Durante's murderer and despite our current differences, I can't see you filling those particular shoes.'

Teddy took a large gulp of his champagne and raised his chin defiantly. 'I heard the whispers that there was something between my wife and Captain Maitland,' said Teddy. 'At first, I dismissed it as gossip, but it only takes one small doubt to creep in and for those doubts to grow before you end up having sleep-less nights. You can't blame a man for wanting to know for certain. I couldn't face the tossing and turning of another night. I borrowed a short metal bar from the hotel's maintenance room and used it to force open the door to Captain Maitland's room. Once in, I found the key to his bureau which I'd previously seen him place on top of the wardrobe and I read his letters and the journal.'

'You had no right,' spat Captain Maitland.

'I had every right, you two-faced rogue. I now know the truth about a man I'd have trusted with my life.'

Captain Maitland turned away. He stared out of the window. Without looking back he said, 'As soon as we return to England you won't need to see me again. On that you have my word.'

Fleming could see how torn Elsie was and he wondered where her feelings truly lay. However, his role in all this was to reveal a killer, not to entangle himself any further in their love triangle.

FLEMING ALLOWED the room to settle for a few minutes before continuing.

Satisfied tempers had cooled, he eyed each guest.

His hand hovered over the pocket watch resting in his waistcoat, his thumb absently following its familiar shape. He gave an inward sorrowful sigh as he summoned his thoughts, and his resolve. He must press on, no matter how distasteful what lay ahead.

He was about to begin when he heard Nancy turn to Fern and say, 'Has Mr Fleming mentioned the ghost yet?'

'It wasn't a ghost, dear,' confirmed Fern.

'The figure you encountered was Durante's killer rushing from the scene of the crime,' said Fleming. 'It's the same person Dolores heard in Durante's room. She heard Durante's door open and close and when she peered out into the hallway she heard the killer running away. She claims she may have heard a second set of footsteps which I believe to have been yours, Nancy, as you returned from your midnight snack.'

Nancy grabbed Fern's arm. 'I might have become a victim too!'

'Now, now. Don't upset yourself. Nothing that happened and you're safe and sound. Why don't you do some more knitting to take your mind off it all?'

'You're right,' said Nancy. 'I'm so lucky to have you, Fern.' She examined her knitting and had soon picked up where she'd left off.

Fleming moved to stand beside Dr Ingrey. 'On the

day of the murder, while awaiting the police, I remained with Durante's body. It provided me with an opportunity to examine his room. I was careful, of course, not to disturb any evidence. It was apparent to me, however, that a search had taken place; there were little details that suggested a disturbance. Naturally, I first thought it must have been our hotel thieves but I came to realise it wasn't them. Whoever had killed Durante had been looking for something in particular. It was during my own search that I came across this.' Fleming turned to Dr Ingrey. 'Would you be so kind as to hold up the evidence, please?'

Dr Ingrey held aloft a finely engraved silver locket suspended on a thin silver chain. 'Inside the locket is a photograph of a young woman and young man. This small piece of jewellery is why Durante was murdered. It's a piece of evidence that the killer knew could expose a dark episode from their past.'

Dr Ingrey rose and handed the locket to Captain Maitland who examined it before passing it on. 'I don't understand. Who are these people? Is this Durante and a woman he loved?'

'It's not Durante,' said Fleming. He held Captain Maitland's gaze before turning to Lord Ernest. 'I've examined every alternative. I gathered my own evidence and considered everything I've learned from information provided by Inspector Trotta on the real reason Durante was here in Venice, I'm afraid my hand has been forced. Would you be so kind as to remove your shoes, Sir Ernest.'

'What?'

'Your shoes. Remove them and place them on the table.' Fleming took a newspaper he had prepared off the cabinet behind him and put it on the table in front of Sir Ernest.

'This is ludicrous.'

'Please humour me,' said Fleming.

With much aggrieved huffing and puffing, Sir Ernest unfastened his shoes and one by one placed them on the newspaper. 'Satisfied?'

'Thank you.' Fleming slid the shoes to the far end of the table next to Dr Ingrey where he examined each one carefully. 'You haven't had them cleaned by the hotel butler?'

'I forgot to put them out to be collected. I know you're a stickler for neatness, Fleming, but I'm assuming dirty shoes aren't a capital crime these days?'

'A shoe can reveal a lot about a man.'

'Is that so?' sniffed Sir Ernest.

Fleming turned each shoe in his hand before placing them back on the newspaper. His attention returned to Sir Ernest. 'I'll admit this leaves a most bitter taste in my mouth. It's time for honesty, Sir Ernest. It's time the truth came out.'

'What does he mean?' asked Lady Templeton. 'What truth?'

Sir Ernest patted her hand. 'Whatever his insinuations, they are of no consequence.'

Fleming thumped the table with his hand. 'Of no consequence!' he bellowed. 'How can those words so easily fall from your lips after what you've done? Despite my already diminished respect for you, my opinion is rapidly sinking further.'

'From now on you had better choose your words very wisely, Fleming,' snarled Lord Ernest.

'I'm scared, Ernest,' said Lady Templeton. 'What's happening?'

'I'm not entirely sure what he's getting at, my love. I think our man Fleming here, has lost his mind.'

'I know the truth, Sir Ernest. A secret that has no doubt haunted you your entire life. The consequences of your actions have impacted too many lives and it stops today. Here and now!'

'What exactly am I supposed to have done?'

'It was you who murdered Durante.'

'Absurd,' scoffed Sir Ernest.

'And before that your lover Sophia Maria Lavigna!'

Sir Ernest's face turned a dark shade of purple. 'Now look here, Fleming. This charade of yours has gone far enough. You're most definitely skating on thin ice.'

Lady Templeton looked pale. 'This is you, Ernest.' The locket had been passed to her and she examined it closely.

Sir Ernest snatched it from her hand and with a pointed finger growled at Fleming, 'You've gone too far, Fleming.'

'Who is Sophia Maria Lavigna?' asked Lady Templeton.

Sir Ernest made no reply.

Fleming lifted his voice to the room. 'Sir Ernest is the young man in the photograph, and at the time the photographs were taken Sophia Maria Lavigna was his lover. The pictures were taken at least twenty-five years ago. In his youth Sir Ernest lived between Italy and England and spent some considerable time in Florence. This was where he met and fell in love with Sophia.'

'You're barking up the wrong tree, Fleming!' Sir Ernest was agitated now.

'But that means it must have been while we were engaged to be married!' Lady Templeton was aghast. The look on her face changed as she considered the facts. 'You travelled a lot in those days. You were gone for weeks at a time. I remember now. I can recall my mother questioning whether you'd ever settle down.'

'The love affair happened before he returned to England, and took up the duties and responsibilities expected of him when he inherited the Swallowbarn Hall estate.'

'This is all complete and utter nonsense,' insisted Sir Ernest. 'What possible reason would I have to kill Durante? I barely knew the man. Or this woman for that matter!' He held up the locket and threw it across the table.

'Sophia Maria Lavigna loved you,' stated Fleming.

'Then why on earth would I kill her?'

'The time came when you had to make a decision. You had reached a point in your life when you were expected to take on the responsibility of Swallowbarn Hall. You were expected to marry. You chose your life in England over her. Unable to face her you wrote to her. In that letter you told her the relationship must end. That it was over, and that you'd never see her again.

'Sophia was distraught. She wrote back and pleaded to see you one last time. Reluctantly, you travelled to Florence, hopeful you could end your love affair amicably and take up your life as an English nobleman.'

'This is all quite extraordinary,' sneered Sir Ernest. 'And absolute tosh.'

'Upon returning to Florence, I suspect you told her you had been forced into an engagement with an English woman. That you had no choice but to marry

Carla. It was what was expected of you. It was your duty. The heartbroken Sophia cried and begged and when you did not relent she threatened to tell anyone who would listen of your life with her. She'd write to anyone with a title in England. You couldn't allow that sort of scandal. It'd jeopardise your position back in England. You argued. Naturally she was angry. She cried. She wouldn't let you go. In desperation she slapped you, called you a coward, sobbed some more, told you she was sorry, that she loved you, and that she knew you loved her. When you insisted you had to leave she wouldn't let you go. That's when the situation got out of hand and in a fit of anger you strangled her.'

Sir Ernest began to laugh. A loud belly laugh. 'If this wasn't so preposterous I'd almost think you were serious. We only have your word the locket ever belonged to me. And besides a photo of someone with a passing resemblance to my younger self, what proof is there I even knew this woman? None, absolutely nothing. And as for Durante. Well, Inspector Trotta has already pronounced it a suicide.'

Fleming waited until Sir Ernest was quite finished. He spoke confidently and assuredly. 'Durante tracked you down through a letter.'

'What letter? There are no letters.'

Fleming retrieved a faded envelope from his pocket

and held it up for Sir Ernest, then everyone else in the room. 'It's the single remaining piece of correspondence between yourself and Sophia.'

'Impossible.'

'Why? Because you thought you'd destroyed them all? After her death her family found this letter hidden among her belongings. In the letter you end the relationship. I wonder whether she hid it on purpose. In case... the worst should happen.'

'A letter like that proves nothing!'

'The letter was written by you. It explains how you must end your love affair. It mentions the locket she gave you. You state you'll treasure it for ever. Several times you repeat you have no choice but to break things off with her. You kept the locket close to you in your study at Swallowbarn Hall, not out of the love you had for her, but out of guilt for what you did to her.'

CHAPTER TWENTY-FIVE

BLUE FLAKE SHOES

S ir Ernest stared fiercely at Fleming. His strong dimpled chin quivered, the veins in his neck stood out. He was unsure how to continue.

'During a conversation I had with Dr Ingrey he mentioned that he'd brought up your relationship with Lord Rossendale,' said Fleming. 'These days a well-respected judge who's presided over several cases of mine. It appears you and he had a falling-out decades ago and your differences have been irreconcilable ever since. I couldn't help but wonder whether there was a connection. I therefore sent him a telegram.'

Sir Ernest clenched his fists. 'He and I were inseparable as young men and went on many adventures together. I'm sure the thrust of his reply was that I should never have married Carla. That she would have been better off with him.'

'He also mentions how deeply you loved Sophia. He knew you'd abandoned her. That and his feelings for Carla were the crux of the disagreement between you. He was unaware, of course, of the heinous crime you'd committed and had assumed Sophia was safe and well, living her life in Florence.'

Sir Ernest shook his head, put a trembling hand to his brow. His breathing had become laboured.

Elsie examined the locket. 'How did Durante end up with the locket if it was in Lord Ernest's possession?'

'Having read the letter which was only recently discovered among Sophia's belongings, Durante travelled to England, in hope of finding out more about Sir Ernest and locating the locket. Durante was the mysterious visitor to Swallowbarn Hall. It was he who, posing as a Professor Bonnard, met you in your study. He disguised his features with a wig, beard, spectacles, and also his voice, which is why his Italian accent was so undetectable. He no doubt made some excuse so that he was left alone in the study for some time, giving him an opportunity to search for the locket.'

'The foreign businessman, Professor Bonnard,' said Dolores. 'The funny-looking man with small glasses, straggly grey hair and a beard. That was Durante?'

'Having seen the locket and now convinced Sir Ernest killed Sophia, the next day he entered Swallowbarn Hall under the cover of darkness and stole it. He then returned to Florence and armed with the find went to Sophia's sister to confirm the likeness.'

'So it was Durante who broke into Swallowbarn Hall, and that was who we'd seen lurking?' said Dolores.

'Indeed it was,' said Fleming. 'You have to remember that Sophia's murder was never solved and it haunted him throughout his career.'

'Why did Durante come to Venice?' asked Elsie.

'Before he could return to England to confront him, Sir Ernest and Lady Templeton embarked on their anniversary trip to Venice. The imminent excursion was something he unquestionably discovered while in Sir Ernest's study at Swallowbarn Hall. So, instead of returning to England Durante booked into the same hotel where he hoped to uncover some concrete evidence. No doubt he wasn't alone in wanting to fully understand more about why Sophia was murdered. I feel certain the family wanted answers too. You see, despite Sir Ernest being the owner of the locket Durante, a thorough and diligent retired detective, wanted more certainty and answers. Unfortunately, when he probed it raised suspicions about Durante's identity in Sir Ernest's mind. Wracked with fear that the truth would come out, Sir Ernest felt compelled to act. He arranged to meet Durante the evening before his death, when Dr Ingrey saw them in conversation. Sir Ernest no doubt hoped he could convince Durante he had the wrong man. However, when he produced the locket, Sir Ernest realised the depth of Durante's determination to prove his guilt. He could feel the noose tightening.'

Teddy had picked up the locket and was examining its back. 'What does the inscription mean?'

Fleming's sharp eyes narrowed in on Sir Ernest. 'It's a phrase I heard you say of Lady Templeton when we first met. Would you care to share its meaning?'

Teddy held the locket towards Sir Ernest but he did not need it. He knew the words by heart. 'It's Italian. It says "*Per sempre nel mio cuore*".'

'What does it mean?' asked Teddy.

'Forever in my heart.'

Lady Templeton gasped. 'That's what you say to me! You've lied to me all these years, Ernest. Everything we had was based on a lie.'

Sir Ernest hung his head. 'I never lied to you, Carla. I simply couldn't tell you the truth.'

'You killed Durante, didn't you?'

'I had no choice. The fool had dedicated his retirement to solving Sophia's murder. He wasn't going to let up, or back off.'

'Who was this woman, this *Sophia*?' Lady Templeton's blue eyes brimmed with tears.

'I loved her. I always have.'

'There's more, isn't there?' said Fleming.

Sir Ernest took a deep breath. 'We had a child together. Years ago, I carefully looked into the infant's well-being and discovered the baby was being raised by her family.'

Lady Templeton began to sob. 'I don't know you at all any more. You're a monster.'

'We've both done things we're not proud of.'

'How dare you! You can't compare my small deception with what you've done. And to think I sold my necklace for us.'

'All these years I've carried this burden and now it's finally over.' He took out his cigarettes and lit one. 'That night I entered Durante's room, I was looking for the locket. He'd told me he had it and I knew it linked me to Sophia's murder. During my search, I discovered a thick file on the case in the deepest drawer of the bureau, along with Durante's old service pistol. I took the file and at first ignored the pistol. I looked everywhere for the locket but couldn't find it. I realised he must have it about his person. I knew then that I had very few options open to me if I was ever going to retrieve it.'

'You chose to kill him and take back the locket.'

Sir Ernest gave a defiant and dismissive wave of his hand. 'Not at first. You have to understand, he left me with very few options. It was him or me. I took his pistol and put it in my pocket. With a letter opener I found on his bureau, I forced off the latch on the shutters leading to the balcony. Then all I had to do was wait for his return. I was going to threaten him with the pistol, force him to hand over the locket. The longer I waited the more I realised that if he refused or overpowered me, or I missed when I fired the pistol, I might not get a second chance.'

'You waited for Durante to return and when he was asleep you murdered him?'

He nodded. 'Using a cushion from the armchair to muffle the sound I shot him. I then made it look like suicide. I put the pistol in his hand and left no trace of my being there.'

'On the contrary, Sir Ernest! You left tell-tale signs that a keen eye could not miss. Like a trail of pebbles they led me through a forest of deceit and confusion directly to where the truth resided. The first clue was Durante's medication at the side of the bed. He would not have prepared his pills before deciding to end his own life; it was therefore not suicide. The cushion missing from the armchair in his room, used to muffle the sound of the shot. It was presumably thrown from the balcony into the canal and washed away. Admittedly, at first the theft of Lady Templeton's necklace overshadowed the real reason for the break-in at Swallowbarn Hall; that was until I understood the necklace hadn't really been stolen at all. Once this piece of the puzzle was solved, I then realised the real reason for the foreign businessman, Professor Bonnard's visit. Then there are your shoes.' Fleming stood beside Dr Ingrey and picked up a shoe. 'The small flecks of blue paint on the floor from the damaged shutters, explain where you hid while waiting for Durante. Of course, you would not have been able to avoid getting a little of the tell-tale blue flakes of paint on your shoes.' He pinched a small blue flake from between the laces and held it up. 'Further examination will find more.'

Fleming raised a hand and in walked the slovenly Inspector Trotta and a sharply dressed constable.

'I heard everything,' said Trotta. He cleared his throat. 'This investigation was a close collaboration between myself and Signor Fleming. Together we solved this case.' Trotta then spoke in Italian to the constable, who hauled Sir Ernest to his feet and led him away in handcuffs.

While Inspector Trotta made further pronouncements about how he'd identified Sir Ernest as a suspect early in the proceedings, Dr Ingrey had to stifle a smile. It was apparent to all that Inspector Trotta had little knowledge of the true facts of the case. However, it was also clear that Fleming was content that Trotta should be allowed to take the credit.

CHAPTER TWENTY-SIX

THE LOCKET RETURNED

Through a series of trains and the hire of a driver, Fleming had arrived in Tuscany at a village on the outskirts of Florence. He'd stopped at a small hotel the previous evening, and after a restorative night's sleep and a light breakfast, he set about his task.

He now took a short break to catch his breath. He'd been informed by two elderly gentlemen, through hand signals and gestures, for he didn't speak Italian and they didn't speak English, that the big house he was looking for could be found at the top of the hill.

The steep and seemingly endless streets were cobbled and lined with pretty, red-tiled, sandstone houses, the morning air filled with the scent of pine and cypress. Admittedly, the magnificent views were a welcome distraction from the effort required to climb the hill.

He took out his handkerchief and mopped his face while he checked the house name on his scrap of paper with the sign on the wall of the building in front of him. *Riposo Celeste*. He folded the paper and put it away.

Fleming was about to ring the bell hanging beside the door when he heard a voice behind him. Gerardo appeared on a bicycle. 'I've been expecting you, Mr Fleming.' He lay the bicycle against the wall, opened a side gate, and together they walked to the rear of the house. 'My aunt and uncle are visiting friends. We'll be alone for a few hours. You look thirsty and exhausted. I'll fetch us drinks. Take a seat in the shade before you collapse.'

Fleming sank gratefully into a chair beneath the canopy of a fig tree. He watched hens at the far end of the garden scratching and pecking at the dirt. A goat tugged at vegetable leaves through a wooden fence.

A few minutes later, Gerardo returned with two glasses of sweet lemonade. Fleming's perception of the handsome, politely spoken young man beside him had changed. He now saw a tragic character. They sat in silence for a while, sipping their drinks, and enjoying the stillness of the afternoon. Fleming placed Gerardo's wristwatch on the table in front of him. 'Nancy and Fern were our hotel thieves.'

'Those two sweet old ladies? I'd never have guessed.' Gerardo chuckled as he fastened the watch to his wrist. 'I assume you've worked out my true identity. I don't suppose you would have come all this way just to return my watch?'

'I became curious when you were vague about where you grew up, and your reason for being in Venice. I heard differing accounts from various guests. It led me to wonder about the inconsistency. At the opera you were attempting to deceive me with your story of Durante and yourself not seeing eye to eye.' Fleming put down his glass and turned to Gerardo.

'I found the deception more difficult than I thought it would be,' admitted Gerardo.

'On this occasion your small lies to hide your identity were understandable.'

'Then you know who I am?'

'You're the illegitimate son of Sir Ernest and Sophia Maria Lavigna. When I learned of the infant left behind after your mother's murder, it was a simple enough matter to trace that child back to your mother's sister and then to you. The age was correct. You resemble your mother, you have her eyes. You took the surname Castelli, that of your aunt and uncle, who raised you after her... demise.'

'Demise makes her death sound too peaceful. He murdered my mother with his bare hands while I slept in my cot in an adjacent room. He then vanished back to England and took up his life as if hers didn't matter. I was found a few days later by a neighbour who happened to come to the house. When he got no reply but heard my crying he raised the alarm. I'm only alive today through sheer luck. They say had it been any longer then I might not have survived either. I was eventually handed over to my mother's family.'

'It's over,' said Fleming finally. 'Sir Ernest confessed to it all and will be judged for what he's done. Your mother can finally rest in peace. You can move on with your life.'

Gerardo forced back tears. 'I'm only sorry Durante can't be here too. What he did in my mother's memory was above and beyond the duty of any police officer. Durante hadn't been a police inspector long when he was given my mother's case to investigate. He promised my aunt and uncle he'd find her killer. He kept his word. I and my family will be attending his funeral. We owe him that and so much more.'

'I'm sure he, his family, and fellow police officers would appreciate that. I, however, must return to England.' Fleming reached into his pocket and handed Gerardo the envelope containing the letter from Sir

Ernest to Sophia, and the locket. 'Durante would want you to have these back.'

Gerardo tucked the envelope into his shirt pocket and opened the locket. 'When did you know I was her son?'

'When I understood Durante's true purpose at the hotel. I soon realised what the two of you were really arguing about when I saw you. He was being protective of you.'

'He thought I might want to exact some revenge on Sir Ernest despite...'

'Despite him being your father?'

Gerardo flinched. 'Yes. Despite him being that.'

'I want you to know I kept our bargain. I didn't tell the other guests who you really are. I imagine it will have to come out when it all goes to court.'

Gerardo examined his mother's photograph inside the locket. 'She came from a traditional and very conservative Italian family. When she fell in love with a foreigner she knew all too well her family would disapprove. She kept their relationship a secret by moving away. They lived in a small hillside farm cottage together. I'm told he would stay for a few days at a time, and they were very much in love. Her family never knew of her affair. The fact she had a child out of wedlock is unthinkable. Sir Ernest must have known that fact and yet he was willing to leave her for his life of privilege in England. He left me, his son! What type of man does that?'

'I'm sorry,' was all Fleming could say.

'I've decided I want him to know who I am. I'm proud of who I've become and I hope my mother would be too.'

'I feel certain she would. Your discovery of the letter made all the difference,' said Fleming.

Gerardo looked satisfied. 'Sir Ernest thought he'd destroyed them all, along with any evidence he'd ever been there. They say the fireplace was filled with ash when the police arrived at the farmhouse. All these years later I was looking through some of my mother's belongings and found it. Seeing what he'd written was hard but I knew it was important. Even though he'd retired, I contacted Durante. I was surprised to discover he was just as passionate about justice for my mother as he'd been in his younger days.'

'It must have been difficult for you to be so close to Sir Ernest in Venice?'

'I will admit I went there with ill-intent in mind. I tried to befriend Dolores as a way to get close to Sir Ernest and Lady Templeton but...' he chuckled, 'she knocked me back at every turn. I wondered whether she had a sixth sense about me, or I simply wasn't her type.'

'Dolores had other matters on her mind. I

shouldn't take her rejection to heart.' Fleming took out his pocket watch. 'I should be leaving. I have a train to catch tonight and a few errands to run before that.' He was about to leave when he reached into his jacket and pulled out a cufflink. 'Yours I presume?'

'Ah, yes. I lost it and I'm not entirely sure where.'

'It was found in Sir Ernest's hotel room.'

Gerardo's face flushed. 'I... I can't lie, I persuaded a maid to let me in, and I must have dropped it when I left the letter.'

'I thought as much.' Fleming waited expectantly.

Gerardo took the hint. 'It was me who sent the anonymous one word letters. The items I enclosed had belonged to my mother. Blue silk ribbon was from her favourite dress, a flower that grew all around the farm-house where they'd lived together, a charred fragment of a photograph recovered from the fireplace. I wanted to torture him for just a little while. Though he denied it, I knew he'd know what each item meant.'

'It's time now for you to move on. You can no longer allow the past to define your future. You have a life that needs to be lived. Go out into the world and make a difference. Even if it's only in a small way. Do some good.'

The two men shook hands.

Gerardo watched as Fleming started down the hill. When he was out of sight he returned to the shady spot beneath the fig tree and sat in silence. After a while, he opened the locket and placed it on the table. He removed the photograph of Sir Ernest, tore it into tiny pieces then let them float away on the gentle hilltop breeze. He closed the locket, kissed it and slid it into his pocket.

CHAPTER TWENTY-SEVEN

PEA AND HAM SOUP

Fleming quietly opened the front door to Avonbrook Cottage and was greeted by the familiar smell of baking. A smile crept across his face. He could hear Mrs Clayton chatting to Skip, his yellow Labrador, in the kitchen. The sound warmed his heart.

'There's no point giving me those huge sad beautiful eyes of yours. If I give you any more cake, you great gannet, you won't be able to move. Then what will Mr Fleming say? Come on, move along now, you're in the way. Why have you pricked your ears? Have you heard something?'

There was the sound of Skip's paws on the tiled floor. Then the creak of the kitchen door.

'Well I never!' exclaimed Mrs Clayton. 'You're home. If I'd known, I'd have come to the train station to meet you. How was your trip? You look like you've been working the fields. Look at the colour of you!'

Before he could answer, Skip jumped up at him barking with excitement, his whole body twisting and turning as he furiously wagged his tail. Fleming patted him. 'Good boy. I'm pleased to see you, too.

'As for how the trip was, well, let's just say it's a joy to be home,' said Fleming.

Mrs Clayton took his hat and coat and hung them on the hall stand. 'As usual, you have a mountain of correspondence to catch up on. Your newspapers are piled up beside your armchair. However, first things first, you look like you need a good meal. I'm sure that Italian food won't have agreed with you. I have some fresh pea and ham soup that'll set you straight. Lewis gathered fresh pods from the allotment this morning.'

Fleming thanked her then winked at Skip when Mrs Clayton headed into the kitchen.

'I saw that,' she said. 'I've got eyes in the back of my head, and don't you forget it. Perhaps I coddle you too much but if I don't look after you then who will? Now, you make yourself comfortable; I'll be a few minutes. I suppose you could do with a proper cup of tea as well?'

'That would be delightful, thank you.'

Fleming left his travel trunk in the hall and went through to the sitting room. Unable to resist, he flicked through the pile of letters to see if any of them caught his eye. He examined a telegram.

'That one arrived today,' said Mrs Clayton, placing a cup of tea on the table beside him. 'I put in an extra spoonful of sugar. I thought it'd do you good. Look at the state of you. You look positively gaunt. I don't know why you do it. Surely, there are enough cases on these shores without the need to traipse all the way to Timbuktu and back.' She tutted and shook her head disapprovingly.

'Venice,' Fleming corrected absently. 'I went to Venice.' He was considering the message in the telegram.

'I know it was Venice. I'm not daft. Before you even consider taking on another case, you're going to have a proper meal. I've made my special Cottage Pie which we can have later. Don't think I don't know you're already considering what your next case should be. I know you better than you know yourself. Now sit down at the table, you're not going anywhere until you've had some of my restorative soup. It'll only be a few minutes.' She could see he wasn't listening so returned to the kitchen.

With a fond smile at her retreating back, Fleming did as he was told. Skip lay down with his head on his paws. Mrs Clayton brought out two bowls of steaming soup and placed them down.

'Now, eat up and tell me all about the goings-on in Venice. There's a Dorset Apple Cake in the oven, I know it's one of your favourites. I trust Countess Volkov is safe and well? You also mentioned in your letter some other business forcing you to extend your stay. And please don't spare me, you know I've become accustomed to the more, shall we say, *lurid* parts of these cases of yours.'

CONTINUE THE SERIES

Thank you for choosing this Henry Fleming mystery. I hope you enjoyed it and will return for The Gravethorn Curse

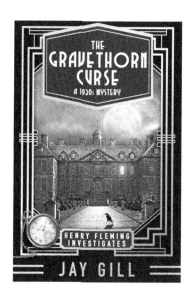

Henry Fleming Investigates

Murder in Fulbridge Village

The Mystery of Watermead Manor

Death on Damson Island

A Deadly Venetian Affair

The Gravethorn Curse

Henry Fleming Investigates (Short Story)

The Theft of the Kingsley Ruby

Inspector James Hardy

Chilling British Crime Thrillers

Caution: This series contains occasional strong language, moderate violence, and mild sexual references.

Knife & Death

Angels

Hard Truth

Inferno

Killing Shadows

Don't Go Home

Inspector Hardy Box Set, Books 1-3

Inspector Hardy Box Set, Books 4-6

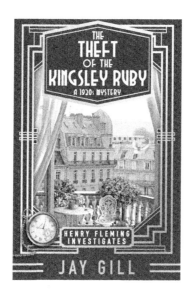

Never miss out, sign up to the newsletter mailing list on my website, and join me on Facebook, Instagram and more.

Jay Gill Newsletter
www.jaygill.net

Facebook Author Page
facebook.com/jaygillauthor

Instagram
instagram.com/jaygillauthor

Twitter
twitter.com/jaygillauthor

TikTok
tiktok.com/@jaygillauthor

Printed in Great Britain
by Amazon

16160439R00161